982

Murder Begets Murder

RODERIC JEFFRIES

Murder Begets Murder

St. Martin's Press
New York

M

794696

Library of Congress Cataloging in Publication Data

Jeffries, Roderic.
  Murder begets murder.

  I. Title.
PZ4.J473Mu [PR6060.E43] 823'.9'14 79-5108
ISBN 0-312-55288-2

CHAPTER I

Babs Browning braked to go from the tarmac road to the dirt track, then drove very carefully in first gear, avoiding most of the potholes but not all. She passed a man ploughing between two rows of orange trees with a mule and a single furrow plough and it pleased her to think that a traveller of centuries ago would have seen very much the same scene, even the design of the plough not having changed.

The dirt track turned sharp left past an outbuilding and here her nose informed her that part of the building was used to house pigs. Someone had once told her that the Mallorquins would only clean out their animals on certain Saints' days because to do so at any other time was to risk having the evil eye cast on those animals: for her money, the smell was the greater danger.

The track turned sharp right at the large estanqui and leading from this was the drystone wall of the terracing down which grew trailing geraniums, one of which bore large variegated pink and white flowers. She stopped the car, climbed out, and carefully nipped off a cutting. Then she saw a bush of wild marjoram, a herb used extensively in local cooking, and she helped herself to some of that. She returned to the car and drove to the end of the dirt track and on to the concrete apron which bordered the lean-to garage and the roughly surfaced patio of Ca'n Ibore.

Along the front of the house was a stone ledge, three-quarters of a metre high, half a metre deep, on which were several pots of geraniums. Their leaves, she noticed, were shot with yellow and their growth was pinched.

There were two sets of front doors, one old and one new. The two old doors were made from solid wood which time and weather had pitted, ribbed, and greyed: the long, thick hinges of rusty iron, fastened by hand-made nails, could have hung doors three times the size and weight; there was a cat hole with swinging flap. The new door, recessed, was glass for half its height and utilitarianly ugly. She knocked briskly on one of the glass panels, turned the handle, pushed the door open and stepped into the hall.

'Betty, it's Babs.'

There was no reply.

'Hullo, hullo, anyone at home?' Betty must be in, surely, since the car was in the lean-to garage.

She heard a sound from behind the nearer of the closed doors on her left. 'Are you in there, Betty? I'm out here, in the hall.'

There was another sound, which she first identified as a whisper but then dismissed this as a ridiculous idea. After a while, the nearer door opened and Betty Stevenage stepped out into the hall, carefully closing the door behind her. She was wearing a gaily patterned cotton dress which did up the front and the top two buttons were undone. Babs looked at the undone buttons, at Betty's flushed face and tousled hair, and finally at her eyes. Babs was a woman of experience and had always prided herself on being able to accept the world as it was, but she was shocked by the certainty that Betty had just been with a man.

'D'you want something?' Betty asked thickly.

Babs liked to help other people, but this didn't stop her usually saying exactly what she thought. But for once she controlled her tongue. 'I came to see how Bill is and if there's anything I can do for you?'

'There's nothing I want.'

'You haven't said how Bill is,' she snapped.

'The doctor says he can't last much longer.'

'I shouldn't pay much attention to that. Doctors are always pessimistic to try to keep their reputations intact.'

Betty was plainly indifferent to that comforting suggestion.

'Well, if there's nothing I can do, I'll go,' Babs said. She crossed to the front door and opened it, then paused. She half turned. 'All those pot plants outside need fertilizing. I'm surprised you haven't noticed it.'

As she returned into the sunshine, warm considering it was early in the year, she realized that she not only felt angry, she also felt degraded, as if she had just taken part in something nasty. But that was quite ridiculous.

She began to walk towards the car, head held high, when she noticed that one of the geraniums was the deep red colour for which she'd been searching for some time: she was surprised she had missed it on her arrival. She nipped off a cutting.

Driving back along the dirt track, she angrily wondered how any woman could become so lost to all standards of normal decency as to be unfaithful to a man who lay dying in an upstairs room?

CHAPTER II

After the sixth glass of wine at a wedding luncheon, Enrique Alvarez usually found himself sadly wondering how long the bride and bridegroom's starry-eyed happiness could possibly last.

There was a loud cheer and he looked the length of the dining-room at the top table where the bride, groom, and their respective parents sat. The groom was holding up a white sheet. Proud the bride these days who had the right to smile demurely when that sheet was held up!

'Cheer up, Enrique,' said Francisca, who sat opposite him on the far side of the wooden trestle table.

His cousin, Dolores, laughed. 'He always looks miserable until the coñac comes round.' She turned to her left. 'Juan, if you eat any more of that pudding you'll be sick: that's your third helping.'

'It's my fourth,' replied her son boastfully. 'Uncle didn't want his so he gave it to me.' He dug his spoon into the caramel custard.

'Let him carry on,' said Francisca. 'After all, it's a wedding . . .'

Alvarez refilled his glass and passed the bottle of red wine across to Jaime, who emptied it into his glass before Dolores could tell him he'd had enough. A waiter, sweating, dressed in open-necked white shirt, blue trousers, and a red cummerbund, began to clear away the dirty plates.

Alvarez lit a cigarette. There must, he thought, be three hundred people eating lunch. Yet the bride's and groom's parents, who'd had to pay for this, were ordinary people. How times had changed, thank God! When his parents had married, they had stopped work in the fields at midday, walked to their respective homes to change into the best clothes they possessed, driven into the town in a donkey cart, been married, and then, after changing back, returned to the fields to work until dusk.

Prosperity had eased people's lives, but it had also destroyed some of their values. When there had been poverty, families had stayed together, neighbour had helped neighbour. Now, married children were no longer willing to have their elderly parents living with them and neighbour overcharged neighbour. Could there never be good without bad: must every coin have two faces?

There was more cheering. One of the groom's friends was cutting his tie just below the knot. A professional photographer took a couple of flashlight photographs, then a third one of the two men cutting the two lengths of tie into dozens of small pieces.

A waiter, carrying four bottles, came to their table and Alvarez chose a brandy. The waiter, who knew him, filled his tumbler. A second waiter brought along a box of cigars and he took one and lit it. If, he thought, Juana-Maria had lived there would have been no feast like this at their wedding because in those days, although the poverty had receded, people had still had to guard their pesetas: but the day would have been no less memorable.

Dolores put her hand on his arm. 'Drink up, Enrique,' she murmured, 'and then have another one.'

He drank, grateful to her for her unspoken sympathy. She was a woman of quick passion, but also of great emotional understanding. Jaime was a lucky man and obviously realized this because he endured his wife's tantrums with, for a Mallorquin, great forbearance.

At the next table, young men were flirting with young

women and making them giggle and blush. Years ago, men and women never tried to behave like that – and if they had, the women's parents would soon have put a stop to such dangerous nonsense. An illegitimate child was a sin beyond understanding. But these days, even in the streets of Llueso, one saw slips of women wheeling prams in which lay their little bastards. They might act as if it were nothing, but surely in their secret minds they must wish times had not changed so that they had not been exposed to temptation.

Juan and Isabel repeatedly asked to be allowed to see their friends who were at a table half-way along the huge room and Dolores eventually said all right, but if they got their new clothes dirty there'd be an infinity of trouble. Isabel, already pert, with flashing dark brown eyes and her mother's jet black hair and beautiful oval face, promised with a saucy grin that they'd be careful. They left.

Francisca leaned forward. 'Now they've gone out of hearing, I can tell you.' She had a small, round face, full of warm good humour but very lined so that there was no mistaking the fact she had known a hard life: her husband had suddenly died after they had been married only six years, leaving her to bring up their son on her own. 'You'll never guess what's happened.' She was a gossip, but most Mallorquins were.

'I know,' claimed Dolores. 'Pedro's being a fool and is insisting on marrying that gipsy woman of his?'

'No, nothing like that. It's to do with the English señor I work for at Ca'n Ibore. He's been ill ever since he came to the island with that English señorita who lives with him.'

'Isn't she blonde and beautiful? You pointed her out to me one day in the square.'

'I suppose some people might describe her like that,'

said Francisca disapprovingly. 'Well, the other day she asked me to buy some pills for the señor: the doctor had told her she must try new ones to see if they would be better. She asked me to buy them and bring them to the house next day. I bought them and went to work for the French señorita in the afternoon and then I began to worry more and more. If the doctor had said the señor must try new pills, why hadn't the señorita driven into the village and brought them back immediately?' Francisca's voice became still more disapproving. 'Well, I worried so much for the poor señor that after I'd got Miguel's supper I bicycled up to the finca so he could have the pills: if she didn't really care about the poor señor, I certainly did! When I got to the finca I propped my bike up against the side of the garage and walked across the patio. That's when I heard them.' She stopped, with histrionic timing.

'Heard who?' asked Dolores.

'The señorita and another man.'

'No! You're making it all up.'

'I'm telling the truth, as God is my witness. They were in the downstairs bedroom. The shutters were shut, but the windows were open because it was a warm night and I could hear them. D'you know what she was saying? She loved him and so he wasn't going to mess around with other women or there'd be real trouble. Just think of it! She was in the downstairs bedroom with a man, talking like that, and the señor was upstairs, so terribly ill.'

'I must say, I thought she looked that kind of a woman,' said Dolores, with the proud complacency of a virtuous woman.

'It made me furious, I can tell you. I banged on the door and she came out of the bedroom looking as if she'd seen a ghost.'

'Had she got anything on?' asked Jaime.

'You would ask that, wouldn't you?' snapped Dolores. Jaime winked at Alvarez.

'Just as if she'd seen a ghost,' repeated Francisca, with satisfaction. 'Then she kind of pulled herself together and shouted at me as if she were mad. She wanted to know what I was doing there. I told her straight, I was worried about the señor suffering, even if she wasn't, so I'd brought the pills up instead of waiting until the next day. That stopped her, I can tell you. She calmed right down and even thanked me for being so kind.'

'Did you see the man?' asked Dolores.

'Not likely. He was much too scared to come out. Men are always cowards.'

'How did the señorita behave the next day?'

'You're not going to believe this, but she was as bold as brass about it. Told me how grateful she was for taking her the pills and what did she owe me, but never a word about the man. That morning I had to take a plate of soup up to the señor. When I saw him lying in bed, with the shutters drawn because sunshine bothers him so much now, his beard and hair needing trimming but nothing done for him because she's too busy . . . I could've wept for him. For two pins I'd have told him just how the señorita was behaving.'

'But you didn't?'

Francisca shook her head.

'There's one thing, he sounds as if he's too ill to worry about what's going on,' said Jaime.

'So,' said Dolores belligerently, 'according to you, when a man is ill his woman's honour means nothing more to him? Then next time you decide you must stay in bed because you sneezed twice and are dying from a cold, I may entertain who I like?'

'You mess around with anyone else while I'm still alive

and you'll end up black, blue and purple.'

'Men!' she exclaimed scornfully, but she would have been happy with no other answer.

A man approached their table, carrying a large tray on which were pieces of the groom's tie and several hundred pesetas in notes and silver – money which would go towards the cost of the honeymoon. 'Come on, now, who's buying?'

Alvarez brought out his wallet from his inside coat pocket and extracted a five-hundred-peseta note. He put the money on the tray and chose a piece of tie. Most people would give only a hundred pesetas, but he felt as if he were lucky enough to be in the position to buy the bridal pair a small piece of marital insurance.

CHAPTER III

Harry Waynton looked at his watch and saw that, even by Mallorquin standards, Diana was late. She so often was. He could never decide whether this was a declaration of independence or a simple inability to be anywhere on time.

A waiter came out of the café and crossed the square to a table where a woman had just joined the couple who had been sitting there. Waynton wondered whether to order another gin and tonic, but finally decided to wait until Diana arrived.

He leaned back in the chair, warmed by the sunshine which was not too hot because the plane trees which grew around the square provided some shade. An American in faded jeans but a startingly bright patterned shirt waved and started to come over to his table, but on the way he stopped to talk to a group at another table and before long he sat down with them. Life on the island was a casual affair, seldom working out as planned. Just right for people who thought life should be enjoyed, not endured.

He remembered how angry, tearfully angry, Gina had been when she sat up in bed in his flat and shouted: 'I want to know what's going to happen to the two of us? Why won't you understand, I've got to know?' He'd tried to explain that tomorrow was a whole world away so forget it, but she'd delivered an ultimatum, either they formed a partnership with a more permanent future planned, or she'd leave him. She was not a woman to back down so, having declared her position, she had had to leave him. He imagined she regretted this as much as he had.

Some men at some stage of their lives ('You're still growing up,' Stephanie had told him, irritated, frustrated, bewildered, by his casual attitude) needed to drift, to let the wind blow them where it would. For them, life needed to be a plethora of different and unexpected incidents.

He'd had a job, at which he'd proved to be very good, working in the PR department of a car manufacturer. Having a strong sense of humour, he'd begun by enjoying his task of trying to convince the great British public that they really should buy British-made cars on the grounds of reliability and quality. But eventually he'd become dismayed by the prospect of spending the rest of his working life dealing in farce.

He remembered Rita, who'd liked to walk naked round his flat because she thought it was so good for skin to 'breathe'. 'I wouldn't,' she'd shouted early one evening and for no reason he could readily discover, 'marry you if you asked me.'

'Why not?' he'd asked, quite interested.

'Because you're so . . . so . . .' She'd struggled to find the right words. 'Irresponsibly casual.' And having spoken her mind, she'd burst into tears and rushed to him to be consoled and he'd wondered about asking her to marry him because she was lovely and great fun, but he'd regretfully come to the conclusion that the world hadn't yet offered him enough experiences for him to settle down.

When he'd handed in his notice, the head of the PR department, a very dependable man, had stared at him in exasperated astonishment. 'Don't you realize, Harry, you're throwing in a job which could take you right up the ladder? And to a thumping good pension.'

How could anyone who was really alive and only twenty-seven worry about his pension?

As he'd wandered through Germany and France, he'd met a number of other people who were drifting before the winds, but most of them, he discovered, seemed to take themselves very seriously. They were, they claimed, searching for meaning. They seemed to view his motiveless drifting with contempt.

In Port Vendres, which he'd reached on a Tuesday when the sun had been shining and the Mediterranean had been a deep, deep blue, he'd discovered that a ferry sailed from there to Mallorca. He'd never been on a Mediterranean island, which was a perfectly good reason for buying a ticket and sailing to one.

He'd seen the concrete jungles, stretches of coast swamped by high rise hotels, apartment blocks, restaurants, tourist shops, and notices which read 'Tea like Mum makes.' He had seen the interior, where gaunt mountains reared up out of a moon-like terrain and black vultures and golden eagles rode the thermals. And he had seen Llueso, nestling on and among hills, not quite untouched by development, yet still master of it.

It wasn't Shangri-la. Just as in anywhere else, there existed indifference, selfishness, hatred, cruelty . . . But it seemed to him as if here man had learned, in so far as he was ever going to, how to live for the greatest enjoyment.

A woman's voice, pitched a trifle shrilly, with a touch of South Kensingtonitis, interrupted his memories and thoughts. 'Hullo, Harry. I saw you sitting here so I thought you wouldn't mind if I joined you for a bit.'

He stood and not for the first time thought what a pity it was that Betty didn't have more taste. She could have been beautiful – an oval face with high cheekbones to hint at feminine mystery, blue eyes, a nose with a suggestion of a turned-up tip, a generous mouth, naturally curly ash

blonde hair, and a slim figure – but she dressed ostenta-
tiously and used far too much make-up. 'Jolly nice to see
you, Betty,' he said and managed to sound as if he meant
it. 'Sit down and tell me what you're going to drink.'

'Can I have a sweet vermouth, please?'

A waiter had come over and Waynton gave the order,
including another gin and tonic for himself. 'How's Bill
today?' he asked as the waiter left.

'He seems to me to be a bit worse, but the doctor says
he's about the same. It can happen any moment.'

'I'm sorry,' he said. He'd never met Bill Heron, who'd
been ill from the day he arrived on the island, and he saw
it as hypocritical to express any more than formally
condolatory words.

She said, very abruptly: 'Are you waiting for someone?'

'I'm meeting Diana here. Although since she's now
well over half an hour late I'm beginning to have grave
doubts on that score.'

'D'you think she's forgotten and gone off with someone
else?'

He shrugged his shoulders and smiled. 'She's over
eighteen so who knows? If so, you've saved me from
getting bored with my own company.'

The waiter brought them their drinks.

A couple came up the steps on to the level part of the
square and looked across to the tables. He knew and liked
them and waved and they waved back and seemed about
to come over when they checked, then turned and crossed
to one of the empty tables to the right. He was fairly
certain they'd decided not to come because Betty was
with him. He wasn't sure whether people merely disliked
her or whether they were reluctant to get close to tragedy:
in the timeless, never-never land of Llueso, the stark
reality of death was thrice unwelcome.

'D'you think she's gone out with Alex?' asked Betty suddenly.

'Who?' he asked, having forgotten what they'd been talking about.

'Diana. Maybe she's having lunch with him and that's why she's forgotten to come here.'

He laughed. 'That's one of the more unlikely combinations I can think up – at least from Diana's point of view.'

'He always tries to be so superior, yet he's nothing to be superior about except he's got money,' she said, with sudden fierceness. 'Keeps making out he's from a big family. He hasn't come from anywhere so why act like he was Lord Muck?'

'D'you think he really does? I know he's a bit pompous at times, but that can be rather amusing.' He'd never understood the resentment which social caste, or the lack of it, or the false assumption of it, seemed to raise in some people's minds.

She said bitterly: 'You know what the trouble is, don't you? People won't have anything to do with me because I'm not married to Bill.'

'Come off it. If not being married were a social stigma, half the couples on the island would be out in the cold.'

'You just don't understand. It's so different for a man: you only think it's amusing. But Bill was going to marry me and then he fell so ill . . .' She finished her drink in three quick swallows. 'God, I'll be glad to get away from this place. Nothing works, the natives rob you every time you open your purse . . .'

'Have another drink and forget it all.'

She might not have heard him. 'The electricity failed a couple of weeks ago and I tried to tell the landlord. He pretended he couldn't understand, so I made him get hold of his wife who speaks a bit of English and told her. It was five days before he came up to see what was wrong. Five bloody days!'

'Time never means much out here. That's surely one of the charms of the place? Except when the electricity doesn't work, perhaps.'

'Charms? God, I've another word to describe what it's like.'

'I'll bet . . . Let's have that other drink and forget all the troubles.' He signalled to the waiter and ordered another round of drinks.

'Bill said that if he died I ought to stay here because I've friends who'll help me. Friends!'

He tried to conceal his irritation at her complaining self-pity.

'I wouldn't stay on here if you paid me to. The moment I've sorted everything out I'm off and I hope it's the last time I ever have to talk to a stuffy, stuck-up expatriate or a sullen native who's only interested in how often he can swindle me.' She picked up her glass, realized it was empty, and replaced it. She was silent for a moment, then she said: 'Maybe she's out with Gordon.' It had been a question, yet she didn't wait for an answer. 'She leads a very social life. Knows everyone. She's lucky.'

If she could have thrown the chips off her shoulder, he thought, she could have started to be lucky. Anyone as attractive as she was needed no social passport.

The waiter brought the drinks and took away their empty glasses.

The clock of the church at the far end of the square struck the hour and as if alarmed by the sound several pigeons rose from the roof of one of the surrounding buildings and, with clattering wings, flew off in the direction of Puig Antonia.

'I'd better get back,' she said suddenly. 'I don't like

leaving Bill for longer than I have to.' She drank so quickly it was impossible she could have enjoyed the vermouth. She left in a flurry of movement, clumsily knocking into a chair at the next table.

Here on the island she was a fish out of water, he thought. Some people never could or would fit into a way of life that was very different from the one they had been brought up in, but he felt certain that even in England she had constantly found cause for discontent.

It was five minutes later, when he'd decided that Diana wasn't coming, that he saw her emerge from the narrow road by the side of the church. She was a striking woman. She wasn't beautiful in the classical sense, but her oval face, framed by jet black hair, was filled with character, suggesting in part her headstrong, sometimes wilful nature. She had a quick, easy smile, but if she were bored she often made no attempt to hide the fact and then her mouth had a disdainful curve to it. She was a person of moods, some of them inexplicable unless one understood that she was looking for something without really being certain what this was. She would accept a quiet, easy life for a time, then would suddenly demand movement and excitement. She could be intensely loyal in friendship, but also cynically critical. She professed a contempt for wealth at the same time as she enjoyed its trappings. The general feeling was that her marriage was bound to have broken up because of her character: but this was based on superficial judgement only.

She crossed the square, aware of the men's interest but contemptuously careless about it. She was wearing a light cotton see-through shirt and tight jeans. She dressed as she felt she wanted to, ignoring the dictates of convention. This was another cause of some people's resentment.

She said, as she sat: 'Am I late?' Her tone of voice suggested she didn't care whether she was or wasn't.

'Far from it. It's not quite half past one yet.'

She looked at him. 'Don't be so bloody accommodating. You know I'm almost an hour late. I got tied up.'

'With Alex?'

'With that PP? Do you mind?'

'PP?'

'Provincial Percy, with emphasis on the euphemism.'

He laughed. 'Then was it Gordon?'

'If you're going to be insulting, at least try to be subtle.'

'They're not my idea. Betty saddled herself on me before you got here and she seemed very interested in who you were with. It's she who suggested either Alex or Gordon.'

'It's a great pity she didn't stay in Southgate, or whatever Godforsaken desert she came from. The men there must just about have been her mark.'

'Don't be too cutting. She was in a bit of a state.'

'Really?'

'Don't you ever feel any sympathy for anyone else? You're in a right royal bitchy mood today.'

She seemed about to reply angrily, then suddenly relaxed. 'You know something, Harry? I think there are times when you're good for me. I always have the feeling that if you get too fed up with me you'll revert to caveman style to vent your annoyance and that keeps me from becoming too obnoxious.' She leaned back in the chair, tilted her head to the sun and closed her eyes. 'I'm late because I ran into Hugh and he wanted to buy me a drink. I was feeling bloody depressed so I accepted. Then I lost count of time. I'm sorry.'

'You realize you've just apologized?'

'I do have my moments of weakness.'

He said, in a neutral tone: 'Hugh seems to be a nice bloke.'

'He is when he stops concentrating on bed.'

'Like that, is he?'

She opened her eyes and looked at him. 'Aren't all men?'

'I can only speak subjectively.'

'And?'

'Yes.'

She laughed.

CHAPTER IV

Francisca pedalled harder, because now the road was slightly uphill. She passed a field, set lower than the road, in which a friend, bent double, was weeding beans. She shouted a greeting. To see someone working in the fields was to be reminded of her husband. He, with her help, had farmed just over ten thousand square metres on a share-cropping basis. The owner of the land had been a real bitch. She'd demanded 50 per cent of all the produce *and* the first choice: the biggest strawberries, the fattest peaches, the juiciest oranges, the densest lettuces, the tastiest artichokes. If she had been content with just a third her husband would not have had to work so hard and then he might have been alive today. But perhaps not. It was impossible for a poor peasant to understand the will of God.

She turned off the tarmac road on to the bouncy dirt track. Miguel, her son, had asked the parents of his girl if he might have permission to call at their house without being invited. Then in four or five years, when they had a home and had furnished it, they would be marrying. How was she going to find the money to provide her share of the wedding feast, like the one Damián and Teresa had been given?

When she rounded the pigsty, she saw that there was a car by the side of the lean-to garage of Ca'n Ibore and a few metres further on she identified this car as Dr Roldán's. Poor Señor Heron. Life could be so unmerciful.

She entered the house, called out, 'Good morning, señorita,' and carried on through the sitting-room to the kitchen.

The kitchen was in a terrible mess, with dirty crockery and cutlery heaped everywhere. Ah well, she was paid to clear up, but couldn't the señorita at least have stacked things? She seemed to be a woman without pride in her house.

After a while the doctor came into the kitchen. 'Good morning, señora.'

'Good morning, señor,' she answered, with the respect due to a man of great education.

'I'm afraid the señor has just died.'

'Merciful Mother of God protect his soul,' she said, and crossed herself.

'Get on your bike and go and tell Arturo Gomez to come up here immediately.'

'Old Gomez? But surely Señor Vazquez is now the undertaker?'

Roldán ignored her.

She took off her apron and carefully folded it up and placed it on one of the chairs.

'Hurry it up,' he said testily.

She had known Dr Roldán's parents well. They had been ordinary villagers, just like anyone else. But their son had been clever and had become a doctor and he'd seemed to think that this made him a different man. Then he'd married a Frenchwoman, beautiful, true, but so expensive. And he'd needed a great deal of money and so had turned more and more to doctoring the foreigners because they paid so much more than the villagers. Now it was as if he had not been born in Llueso, but had come from afar. Ah well, that was the way the world turned.

She bicycled back along the bumpity dirt track. She was surprised she was to call in Arturo Gomez, who had had precious little work over the past few years because people now went to Vazquez who had expensive coffins

and the biggest car in the village to carry the coffin in ...
Señor Heron could not have been nearly as rich as she'd
always imagined. Would there, then, be any money for
the señorita? She wasn't the kind of woman who would
know how to live on little. Or perhaps she was thinking
only of the money and that was why she was denying her
lover the kind of funeral that would have honoured his
memory.

Over one hundred people attended the funeral of William
Miles Heron. The English vicar, from Palma, read the
burial service and the very plain coffin was lifted by four
men into the sepulchre where it would stay for seven years
before being opened so that the bones could be removed
and buried in the corner plot of land reserved for heretics.
Betty Stevenage asked all the mourners back to a funeral
tea at Ca'n Ibore. None of the wealthy or the socially
elite accepted the invitation because they had shown the
necessary respect towards the dead and they did not wish
there to be any confusion about their feelings towards the
living.

CHAPTER V

June was a month of constant sunshine and each day the thermometer reached a little higher until all previous temperature records had been broken. During the day the holidaymakers in their hundreds lay and sunbathed and during the evening they suffered from sunburn. It was ideal weather for doctors, chemists, soft drinks and ice-cream manufacturers.

José Sanchéz's only response to the unusual heat was to drink more. His wife frequently called him a drunken lay-about, good at nothing but swilling and gambling in the bars, but as he invariably replied, perhaps after a blow or two to quieten her down, it was his money so no one was going to stop him doing what he wanted with it.

He'd always been a lucky man. Almost from the day he'd been born, his father had recognized him as being a lazy good-for-nothing. His father had known when death was coming, so he'd taken great care to see that each of his three sons obtained his just deserts. To his wife he left his house in the village, to Adolfo and Bernado his land because land was more valuable than gold and they were wonderful sons, to José he left the half-ruined house on one of the fields because the law said he must leave something to each of his children and that was the most worthless thing he possessed. He hadn't been dead a year when foreigners began to arrive on the island, all searching for somewhere to buy or rent. One day a ruin was worth just a few pesetas, the next (or so it seemed) hundreds of thousands, even millions. Before long José Sanchéz's house was worth so much more than his brothers' fields that he laughed every time he watched them laboriously tilling the soil.

Instead of succumbing to the lure of a million pesetas, which was the sum a German offered him for the broken-down Ca'n Ibore, he'd persuaded a builder to reform the house, using the cheapest available materials. Naturally, he never paid many of the builder's bills. When the house was finished, he'd offered it at a rent which all his acquaintances delightedly told him was much too high – and a simple foreigner paid it. At the end of that first let he'd raised the rent and all his acquaintances had rushed to tell him that now he was just being completely crazy – and another simple foreigner paid it, again without even trying to haggle. And these inflated rents were all profit because he'd discovered how to avoid all maintenance costs. When the tenants complained because the plaster peeled off the walls, shutters fell, the water-pump burned out, the water-heater failed, the water supply became clogged up with muck from the estanqui which he was too lazy to clean, and the worm-eaten furniture collapsed, he merely failed to understand what they were shouting about and in the end, in desperation, they usually themselves paid to have the repairs effected.

He drove up to Ca'n Ibore in his battered, ailing car, not quite as happy as he usually was when he approached the house that was his. Annoyingly, in a way one of the foreigners had managed to get the better of him; or, to be strictly honest, he had failed to take the foreigner for quite as much as he ought to have been able to. The man had died and the woman had said she was leaving the island, so everything had been set for his regaining possession of the house inside the period of the lease (paid in advance). But then the woman, with deplorable stupidity, had handed the keys of the house to her solicitor and said that the landlord was not to be let into the place until the term of the lease was up. A mean, spiteful action.

He unlocked the front door and stepped into the hall. Mother of God, what a stink! Was this how the English left a beautiful house which they'd rented? It would take days to get rid of the smell and this was when the high season was almost on them and a Frenchman or a German might be persuaded to pay as much as eighty thousand a month.

He went into the sitting-room. The dining-table, down by the window, still had on it the remains of a meal. Couldn't even be bothered to clear up! Still, he'd demanded a deposit of five thousand pesetas against breakages and one could put up with a lot of stink and disorder for five thousand.

He pushed open the swing door of the kitchen and almost recoiled, because here the smell was nearly overpowering. When he looked to his left, past the antique dresser, he saw what was causing the smell.

CHAPTER VI

Alvarez, sitting behind his desk, stared at the shaft of sunshine coming through the window in which was a multitude of dancing flecks of dust. It was tiring to watch such ceaseless activity.

The internal phone buzzed. He ignored it and continued to stare at the dancing dust. Eventually, each single speck would end up on the floor, lifeless. Most of what a man did during his lifetime ended up forgotten. So relax . . . Eyelids closed and his mind slipped into a delightful peace

The internal phone buzzed again, jerking him wide awake. Resentfully, he lifted the receiver.

'It's taken you long enough to answer.'

The captain of the post had never learned to relax, undoubtedly because he came from Madrid. 'I was tied up with some work, señor.'

'There's a report in of an Englishwoman who's been found dead in a finca. The address is Ca'n Ibore. That's in La Huerta. Get out there and find out if it's a matter for investigation.'

He replaced the receiver, then slowly stood up, yawned, and looked down at his stomach which was straining his trousers. He kept telling Dolores he shouldn't eat so much, but like all good cooks she became annoyed if he seemed not to appreciate her food. Also, when a man grew older there were few pleasures left to him and so these became doubly precious.

He left the room and went downstairs. His car was two roads from the post and by the time he reached it he was sweating and a bit short of breath. Perhaps he should take up some form of exercise? Tomorrow, he assured himself.

He loved Ca'n Ibore from the moment he turned the corner by the pigsty and saw it above the orange trees. It was the kind of house he would buy if ever fate made a mistake and showered him with favours. Built with rocks gleaned from the fields, it was as much a part of the land as the trees which grew around it.

He parked by the side of the lean-to garage and as he climbed out of the car Sanchéz came hurrying up the stone steps which led down to the terrace below the patio. His face was strained and when he spoke his voice was hoarse. 'She's in the kitchen. She . . . She . . .' He shook his head.

'Are you sure she's dead?'

'God Almighty, am I sure! I've never seen anything so terrible.'

'Have you called for a doctor?'

'I haven't done anything but tell the Guardia. Why's it happened to me? Why did she – '

'How long d'you reckon she's been dead?'

'I don't know. How can I know?'

'You must have some idea,' said Alvarez, trying to make Sanchéz calm down.

Sanchéz looked resentfully at him, but when he next spoke he was more coherent. 'The señor rented the house for six months. Then he died and the señorita said she wasn't going to stay, but she wouldn't give me the keys, she gave them to the solicitor and said I wasn't to have 'em until the six months were up and the lease was over. He gave them to me today. When I went inside, I found her.'

'How long ago did the señorita hand over the keys to the solicitor?'

'Roughly a month.'

Alvarez fingered his thick, square chin for a moment, then said: 'If she gave the keys to the solicitor, how come she was inside with the door locked?'

'I don't know, do I? Why keep asking me?'

'Was there a spare front door key?'

'I didn't give 'em one.'

'What about the back door?'

'Locked and shuttered. And all the windows are shuttered.' 794696

'You've checked on 'em all, then?'

'It's my house. It was empty. Why shouldn't I check?'

'All right, I'm only asking. Let's go on inside.'

'Not me. As God is my witness, I can't go back in there . . . She's in the kitchen, beyond the sitting-room. She's on the floor and . . .' He gulped.

Alvarez looked at him, shrugged his broad shoulders, then opened the door. The smell was quite appalling. Once inside he turned and looked at the door and he saw what Sanchéz had missed – a key with a length of string threaded through the small hole in its end, carefully hung where no one could smash one of the panes of glass and reach it. That explained the door, then: they'd wisely had a spare key made and it had been kept there.

At the far side of the hall were stairs, which turned a half circle, and under them an archway into the sitting-room. He went through. To his left now was a swinging door and he pushed this open to enter the kitchen. She lay on the floor between a table and the antique dresser, arms outstretched, right leg curled up under her.

When he returned to the patio he stood in the sun and drew great draughts of sweet, fresh air down into his lungs.

Sanchéz came up to where he stood. 'What are we going to do?'

'You are going into the village to the Guardia post and you'll ask someone to telephone Palma and call the police doctor to come out here as quickly as he can make it.'

Sanchéz turned and hurried across the patio to his car.

Alvarez lit a cigarette. He looked up at the grape vine which covered most of the patio, then out at the orange grove, the almond trees beyond, at Puig Antonia on the top of which, as near to Heaven as the builders could get, was the hermitage, at the mountains which ringed Llueso, and at the bay, part of which was just visible as a thin streak of blue seen through a gap in the trees. So much beauty, but behind him so much ugly corruption. Always there seemed to be two faces to life.

Ever since he had arrived the name of the house had been worrying him because it had seemed as if he should recognize it. Now, as he turned away from the beauty of the view, he remembered why Ca'n Ibore was familiar. Francisca had been talking about it at the wedding of Damián and Teresa. Then it was the señorita who had loved a man even while the señor who loved her was dying in his bed upstairs who now lay dead in the kitchen.

Back in the house, he examined the two bedrooms and bathroom to the right of the hall. None of the beds was made up. In the bathroom there was soap by the bath and handbasin, a single towel on the rack by the basin, and a face flannel on the rack between bidet and bath. In the bathroom cupboard three of the four shelves were empty, on the fourth were a tin of powder, a bottle of aspirins, a deodorant applicator, an electric toothbrush, and toothpaste.

He climbed the semi-circular staircase which brought him to a large solar, empty except for two wooden chests, both badly worm-eaten. One chest was filled with bed linen, all carefully folded, the other was empty. Beyond were two bedrooms, separated by an impractically small bathroom. The back bedroom had an unmade-up double bed and a small built-in cupboard which was empty. The front bedroom had a single bed, made up, under the pillow of which was a flowery nightdress, a bedside table on which was an alarm clock, a paperback, and an adjustable light. There were only a few clothes in the cupboard, but on the floor was a packed suitcase and another half-packed.

He returned downstairs to the sitting-room. Beyond the main part of this was a well, used as the dining area. The table had been set for one person and on it now was a plate filled with empty mussel shells and a quarter of lemon, another large plate with dried-up remains on it, a side plate, a loaf which was rock hard, a plastic container which had once contained butter, a slab of cheese which had grown mould and then dried right out, an earthenware bowl in which was a slime which had been lettuce leaves in oil and vinegar dressing, and a half-full bottle of wine with a thick crust. He opened the window, then the shutters, and sharp sunshine streamed through.

He went into the kitchen and hurriedly opened the window and the shutters. In the door of the main body of the refrigerator was only one bottle of milk, half-full; the door of the frozen compartment was blocked by ice. He looked in the larder. Everything was stacked up, ready to be left. He checked the drawers on each side of the sink and these were either empty or they contained cutlery or drying-up cloths. In the right-hand side of the double sink was a saucepan in which the mussels had been cooked. He pulled open the two doors beneath the sink. Inside the space were bottles of washing-up liquid, bleach, and Ajax, and two buckets, one of which contained a small amount of wastepaper and the other a number of empty mussel shells and a quarter of lemon.

He returned to the patio, sat down on one of the metal chairs, smoked, and luxuriated in the fresh air and the sunshine, dappled by the vine leaves. There was the distant, muted sound, almost a whisper, of the hour being struck by one of the three church clocks, then seconds after the last stroke he heard the crackling, crushing noise of a car approaching along the dirt track. A red Renault 4 turned the corner by the building which was part pigpen.

Sanchéz parked and came over to where Alvarez sat and it was immediately obvious that, with the help of a few brandies, he had regained some of his normal cockiness. 'I've done that for you, then. What I want to know now is what happens next?'

'We wait.'

'I can't afford to wait for long and that's a fact. I need the house clear. This is prime letting time, you know, but it won't be any use me showing anyone over the house until the body's away and the stink's gone.'

Alvarez looked at him with scorn, but Sanchéz was quite unconcerned: there might have been a sad and tragic death, but one could not afford to be sentimental where money was concerned.

CHAPTER VII

Francisca González lived on the west side of Llueso, in a small house on what had been the main Palma road before the new by-pass had been built. Alvarez stepped into the first room, which was the formal sitting-room as well as, from necessity, the hall, and he called her name. She came hurrying into the room, her lined face creased with a welcoming smile.

'Enrique! What brings you here at this time of day? Are you thirsty?'

'I'll not say no to a coñac, the bigger the better.'

She looked curiously at him, realizing with some disappointment that this was not just a casual social visit. 'Come on through and pour out however much you want.'

The second room, the same size as the first, was used as a dining-room and the family sitting-room. She pointed to an elaborately panelled sideboard. 'The bottles are in the left-hand side and the glasses are in the right.'

As she sat, he poured himself out a very generous brandy. 'D'you remember Teresa's wedding?' he asked. He drank eagerly: when a man felt the warmth spread through his stomach he knew for certain that he was still alive.

'Of course I remember it. Matter of fact, I saw her and Damián only yesterday and they asked me up to their flat. It's wonderful to see how happy marriage makes people.'

He crossed to a chair and sat. He was not unaware of the fact that both she and Dolores thought that a marriage between himself and her would be a very sensible arrangement. But as much as he liked and respected her, he liked his freedom more: when a man had had his freedom for a long time, it was difficult to think of giving it up in any but exceptional circumstances. 'During the meal you told us about Señor Heron, who was very ill, and Señorita Stevenage who lived with him.'

'The poor señor,' she said. 'He'd suffered so much before he died.'

'Matter of fact, I'm just back from Ca'n Ibore. The lease was up today and so the landlord, José Sanchéz, was able to go inside. He found that something very awful had happened. The señorita had died in the kitchen.'

'Mother of God!' she exclaimed with horror. Then she looked disbelievingly at him. 'How could she be dead when she was so alive the last time I saw her? How can she have died and no one know about it?'

'I'm here to try and find out. Can you spare the next half-hour?'

'I'm not going anywhere, Enrique. I haven't been able to find work in the mornings since I left Ca'n Ibore: the foreigners say they haven't the money they used to and when I ask for another ten pesetas an hour they tell me they can't afford that much. But all the time the prices go up and up.' She spoke with fatalistic acceptance.

'Tell me now, then, how you first went there and what happened.'

Carmen had come to her in December and said that there were some foreigners in Ca'n Ibore who wanted a maid in the mornings. So she had bicycled up to the finca to see them. The poor señor was ill, but no one could mistake him for anything but a gentleman, so kind and pleasant, so distinguished in his smart clothes, well trimmed beard, and greying hair even if he wasn't very old. And to think she hardly ever saw him again except in his bed of pain! But the señorita . . . How did an unmarried woman so degrade herself as to live with a man? Not so

long ago she would have been called a whore . . .
'You told us you thought she was having some sort of
an affair with another man, didn't you?'
'Indeed I did! The poor señor, dying upstairs, and her
downstairs telling another man how much she loved him!
I have to say it after all, Enrique: she was a wicked,
wicked woman. Look at the way she always tried to make
out she cared so much for the señor. I'd offer to take him
something to eat, she'd insist on carrying it up because he
wanted to see her and he needed her. But there were no
tears in her eyes when she spoke about him: her soul was
not being squeezed. Yet when her little dog died – then
there were tears! She cried as if her heart were broken.
So I tell you, she loved her dog more than the señor.
Imagine!'
'The English are funny over their animals.'
'The señor loved her. But she . . . she was glad when he
died.'
'After a long illness it can be a release for anyone.'
'Maybe. But why didn't she really do something for
him? Make him see a specialist in Palma, make him enter
a clinic, where they could perhaps have helped him? If it
had been my man I'd have done everything possible for
him.'
'The doctor surely tried to get him to see a specialist or
enter a clinic?'
'Doctor Roldán? He worries about nothing except that
his enormous bills are paid so that he can buy that French
wife of his another frock.'
'Tell me again what happened that evening you collected the pills from the chemist and decided to take them
to the house right away instead of waiting until the morning.'
'She said not to bother until the morning. How could

anyone not bother when the señor was so very ill? You'll understand, Enrique, that when I left the dirt track and was on the concrete I made no sound. So they could not have heard me, but when I drew level with the window I could hear her all right.'

'Can you remember exactly what was said?'

'Not every single word, but some of them I shan't forget in a hurry. She wasn't shouting, but her voice was very strong when she said: "I love you. Don't you ever forget that." Then she told him she wasn't going to sit back and let him mess around with other women. He said something which I couldn't understand because he was speaking in such a low voice, then she told him that she knew he was trying to mess around with other women and if he didn't stop it, she'd make trouble for him.'

'Did you get any idea of who the man was?'

She shrugged her shoulders. 'He was speaking so quietly. It could have been any foreigner.'

'So what happened when you let them know you were around?'

'When she came out of the bedroom she began to shout, wanting to know what I was doing spying round the house at that time of the evening . . . I said, very quietly, "Señorita, I have brought the señor's pills because he may need them during the night." She just grabbed them from me. "Señorita, there were sixty-seven pesetas more to pay than you gave me." "You'll get the money tomorrow – now clear off." '

'Charming! What was she like the next day?'

'There was quite a change, I can tell you. "Thank you so much for bringing up those pills. I was ever so grateful. I'm sorry I made such a fuss, but I was so worried." Then she looked at me out of the corners of her cat's eyes and said: "A friend of mine came up last night and gave me

some rather bad news. That's why I was so very upset.'
A friend! As if I didn't know what kind of a friend she was
talking about. And another thing, I reckon she was trying
to find out, without actually asking, how much I'd heard.
I wouldn't let on, of course.'

'What happened after the señor died?'

'She said she wasn't staying in a country where everyone swindled her – how many times have I done things
for her, yet never charged? – and that as soon as possible
she was leaving. Just before she left . . .' Francisca stared
worriedly at Alvarez. 'I mean, just before she was supposed to leave, she paid me an extra week's money and
that was the last I saw of her.'

'Do you know exactly when she planned on leaving?'

'She paid me on a Tuesday and said she was going the
next morning after breakfast.'

'What time on Tuesday was it when you last saw her?'

'It was just before lunch, which was my usual time for
leaving.'

'Have you any idea what she was going to eat for
lunch?'

'But what can that matter?'

'It just may do. Think back and try to remember.'
She stared at the empty fireplace, decorated with some
fir cones which had been painted silver and gold, and after
a while she said: 'It must have been some kind of lamb
because I had to pick the mint. D'you know, they always
put mint and vinegar on lamb when they eat it.'

'She wasn't having mussels?'

'There weren't any mussels around.'

He finished his brandy and then began to twirl the
stem of the glass between his finger and thumb. 'Have you
ever seen her with any men other than the señor?'

She shook her head. 'Never.'

'Did people visit the house very much?'

'Hardly anyone. But if she hadn't been there, then I'm sure lots of people would have come to see the señor.'

'Can you suggest any of their friends I can talk to? Perhaps someone who you know has visited her more than once.'

After a while she said: 'Señora Browning used to come quite often to see if she could help. But even so the señorita was always rude about her.'

'Do you know where this señora lives?'

'I'm sorry, Enrique, but I've no idea.'

'No matter. I'll find out.' He put down the empty glass. 'Thanks a lot for all your help. I suppose I'd better start moving on.'

'Now – when it's almost time for lunch? Stay and have a bite? I've made paella, because Miguel likes it so much, with some specially large prawns.'

When a man started putting his feet under the dining-table of a widow . . .

'And for afterwards I've some tripe in the way my mother used to bake it.'

Tripe, when well cooked, was a food for the gods. He slowly settled back in the chair.

She smiled contentedly. 'Give yourself another drink while I go through to the kitchen and carry on cooking.'

He poured himself another, and even larger, drink.

CHAPTER VIII

The Mobylette slowed right up as the slope steepened and Waynton finally jumped off it, walking beside it for the last hundred metres up to the turning into the small entrance courtyard of Ca Na Ailla. As he swung off the road he saw a white Seat 127 which he identified as Hugh Compton's. He swore.

He pulled the Mobylette up on to its rest, crossed to the front door, and rang the bell. Diana opened the door. 'Hullo, Harry. Come on in and join the party. Hugh dropped in a bit earlier.'

He was pretty certain there was a malicious smile lurking about her lips. From her point of view, why not? They went into the sitting-room which, because the house was built on the side of the mountain, had a magnificent view over the land to the mountain-ringed bay. Hugh Compton, who was sitting out on the terrace, sounded really pleased to see Waynton. 'It's good to meet you, Harry. I was saying only yesterday to Tom that I hadn't seen you around for a bit, which was a pity because out here when an intelligent man goes missing he leaves a big gap.'

How to make all your acquaintances love you, thought Waynton. Then he laughed at himself for this un-characteristic small-mindedness, knowing its cause was jealousy. Jealousy that Diana obviously liked Hugh, jealousy because the gods had been so kind to him. He was crisply smooth and ruggedly handsome. He had plenty of money: he could charter a yacht and take Diana out sailing, then dine at the fish restaurant in the Port without wincing when she said she'd rather like lobster. And most of all, he had a warmth of character which enabled him to make friends with almost everyone, even the dragon of a dowager duchess who came over to the island and lived in the Port whenever she was temporarily broke.

Diana indicated a trolley just inside the sitting-room. 'Help yourself to what you'd like, Harry. There should be ice in the container: if it's melted, there's plenty more in the fridge.'

He poured himself out a gin and tonic and added lemon and three cubes of ice. He sat.

'I went to Ray's party last night,' said Hugh Compton. 'I do wish he'd stop putting sixty-peseta gin into old Gordon bottles and then serving it with a flourish. That sort of thing should only be done with discretion.'

'When I first arrived out here,' said Diana, 'I was warned about him on two accounts. Never drink gin in, or express an interest in, his home.'

'I know the consequences of drinking his gin. What happens if he gives you an escorted tour?'

'If you're a female it's a hand round the waist in the dining-room, a loving nip on the bottom in the kitchen, and a free-for-all in the first bedroom.'

'Never tell Norah that or she'll rush to see all the other bedrooms as well.'

She laughed. 'You're very cruel about her.'

'She loves suffering. It's her Slavonic blood.' He turned his wrist until he could see the face of his gold Rolex. 'I suppose I'd better start shifting.'

'Don't rush. Stay and have another drink?'

'I'd love to, but I made the grave mistake of saying I'd have a pre-lunch pick-me-up with Alice and Brian.'

He stood up, broad-shouldered, narrow-waisted, dressed in casual clothes which would never be mistaken for cheap. 'So long, Harry. Come and have a noggin the next time you've a spare moment. I promise to leave the sixty-peseta gin tightly corked up.'

After they'd left, Waynton stared out across at the bay and wondered what degree of friendship there was between Diana and Hugh. It always seemed light, but he remembered Diana telling him that Hugh's thoughts, like Ray's were constantly turned towards bed.

Diana returned through the sitting-room and came out on to the balcony. 'I was so fed up with my own cooking that I'd decided to go out for lunch. Let's go Dutch to Ca'n Mercer?'

'Make it English style and you've got a date.'

'I said Dutch. Take it or leave it.'

'Knowing you, I suppose I'll just have to take it.'

'Right. Pour yourself another drink whilst I go and freshen up. And if you'd like an olive, there's a tin of stuffed ones on the kitchen table which I was going to open but never got round to.'

He poured himself a second drink, then returned to his seat, not bothering about the olives. He admired an independence of spirit, but sometimes wished that she didn't possess quite so much of it – or, at least, that she had learned to deploy it less challengingly. There were times when a man liked to feel that he was leading, even if he were too blinkered to see that in reality he was being led . . .

The front-door bell rang.

'Harry, go and see who it is, will you? I'm not in a fit state to be seen in public.'

He went through to the front door.

'Hullo, there,' said Jerry Crutchley in his gobbling way of speaking which matched his turkey face and wattle chins. 'We didn't expect to see you here, did we, Vi?' His small, very dark brown eyes were bright with enquiring interest.

His wife, a tired blonde, didn't answer him: she seldom did.

'We came because we wondered if Diana had heard the news,' said Crutchley.

Waynton opened the door more fully. 'Come on in and find out. She'll be along in a second.' One might as well try to keep the tide at bay as keep the Crutchleys out in the cold during drinking time.

They had nearly finished their drinks when Diana appeared. Her greeting, since she could rarely be bothered to dissemble her feelings, was cool. But the Crutchleys noticed nothing, perhaps because they were used to such a reception.

'I said to Vi, didn't I, Vi, I wonder if Diana's heard the news?'

His 'wife stared down into her glass.

'Basil told us about it.'

'Then it's bound to be true,' said Diana.

He was impervious to sarcasm. 'Betty Stevenage has been found dead in the house that she and Bill rented. She'd been dead a long time and was in a bit of a state,' he added, with grisly pleasure. He drained his glass and then held it in a conspicuous position.

'For Heaven's sake!' said Diana. 'You'd believe the end of the world had happened if someone told you it had. Betty went back to England as soon as everything was cleared up after Bill's death. It must be a month ago now.'

'But that's just the point, Diana, she didn't leave. We all thought she did, but in fact she died very suddenly in the kitchen and has been lying there ever since. Just think of it – lying in the kitchen, dead!'

'If this were true,' said Waynton, 'surely someone would

have discovered her body long before now?'

'That's just what I thought. But apparently Bill and Betty had had nothing but rows with the landlord who'd never do any of the repairs that were needed and after Bill died Betty went and saw one of the solicitors in the village and left him the keys of the house and told him not to hand them over until the very last day of the lease. She'd obviously locked up for the night using a spare key, shutting all the shutters, and all that sort of thing, so no one could get into the place. The landlord hadn't the slightest idea of what had happened.'

'She must have made arrangements to stay somewhere in England or wherever she was going. They'd have started to worry when she didn't turn up.'

'Perhaps she'd only booked in at a hotel, so they'd just think it was a cancelled reservation. I hate to be beastly to anyone, but she really wasn't the kind of person who could easily make friends, was she, so perhaps there's no one in England who cared whether she returned, or not: or even knew she was meaning to.'

'I suppose it's possible. But then what's she supposed to have died from?'

'Basil didn't know.'

'He's slipping,' said Diana scornfully.

Crutchley smiled, a little uncertainly. 'As I said to Vi – didn't I, dear? – it really is too tragic for words. Bill dies after a long illness and then she dies so soon afterwards with no one knowing. Really tragic.'

'Do stop rolling out the platitudes,' snapped Diana. 'There's nothing more tragic about dying and lying around the place for a month than just dying. And a couple who die soon after each other are a damn sight luckier and less tragic than a survivor who goes on year after year, alone.'

Crutchley stared at her and seemed to be about to say

something, but in the end he merely made a gobbling sound. Nonconformity, in thought or action, always disturbed him.

'I'll have to ask you to drink up,' said Diana. 'I'm sorry to rush things, but we're just on our way out.'

He looked astonished. Not even one refill?

The heat of the afternoon had eased by the time Alvarez awoke. For a while he remained motionless, sprawled out in the chair, then with a grunt of resigned annoyance he opened his eyes. He stood up and crossed to the shutters to open them. When the harsh sunlight streamed in he had to blink rapidly to ease his eyes. He looked down at the street in which the only living thing at that moment was a dozing cat and he yawned, envying the cat.

He walked from the post to the square, where a large number of tourists were sitting out at the tables, and threaded his way through the narrow streets to the solicitor's office. The receptionist said Señor Vives was out seeing a client, but would be back at any moment. Alvarez slumped down in a chair, which squeaked at the weight of his thickset body, and thought about nothing in particular.

When Vives arrived, looking very smart in a light-weight suit, he greeted Alvarez warmly, led him into his office, and pulled round a comfortable chair in front of his large desk which was covered with files, books, and papers.

'Now, then, Enrique, what's brought you here? Some-body not paying one of the new taxes the government keeps introducing?' He laughed. The stupidity of men in far-off Madrid who seemed to think they could rule the lives of the fiercely independent islanders was a constant source of amusement.

'I'm trying to check up on the Englishwoman who's been found dead in Ca'n Ibore. Were you her solicitor?'

Vives's very mobile face became solemn. 'Poor Señorita Stevenage. Yes, I acted for her and Señor Heron, before he died.'

'It seems she must have died about a month ago. How come she wasn't discovered before now?'

'It's easily explained, Enrique.' He spoke about the trouble there had been with the landlord, Sanchéz. 'She told him what she'd done with the keys and on the Wednesday afternoon after she was supposed to have left the island he was in here, pleading with me to let him have them – only so that he could go inside and see everything was all right: promised on the honour of his mother, grandmother, and great-grandmother, that he'd do no more than that.' Vives chuckled. 'If I'd given him the keys there would have been new tenants in the house just as soon as he could find them. And paying four times a reasonable rent.'

'There's a fool born every minute.'

'When it comes to foreigners on this island, the birth rate's obviously even higher than that. Listen to what happened this morning! An English señor comes in here in a terrible state, begging me to help him. He came to the island in Easter for a week's holiday – remember how lovely Easter was? – and falls in love with everywhere. So he decides to buy a house down in the Port. An odd-job man says he knows a beautiful house for sale, a perfect bargain at only two and a half million. Does the Englishman seek advice from a lawyer, as he would have done in his own country? No! He paid without asking a single question. And now he's discovered that the land is owned by three brothers, one of whom lives in Argentina and refuses to sell, the house was put up by a builder who never

bothered to buy the land, he mortgaged the house to a
bank, then went bankrupt, and the bank is going to
foreclose.'

'So what happens to the Englishman?'

'He has almost certainly lost two and a half million
because there were blue skies at Easter. It can be a cruel
world, Enrique.'

'Getting back to the señorita – have you any idea how
she intended to get from Ca'n Ibore to the airport?'

Vives pursed his lips. 'I certainly can't be certain, but I
do seem to remember she said she was ordering a taxi.'

'I'll have to see if I can find the driver.' Alvarez pulled
himself out of the chair and stood. 'There's one last thing. I
want a word with a Señora Browning. You wouldn't know
where she lives, would you?'

'Ca Na Penoña,' Vives answered immediately. 'The
house is in the entrance to the Festona Valley . . . Now if
you're talking about rich foreigners, you're talking about
her. Marry her and you'd not have to worry about where
your next meal was coming from.'

'I'd rather go hungry.'

Vives laughed. 'A man of principles: expensive principles!'

Alvarez left and returned to the square, where he spoke
to the drivers of the three taxis which were parked there.

The last driver said: 'Yes, I remember her. She came
and booked me to take her to the airport.'

'Have you heard that she's just been found dead in the
house?'

'Mother of God!' exclaimed the driver, and crossed
himself.

'I want a word with you and this car's like an oven.
Come on over to the club.'

'But what if a fare turns up?'

'Tell him to wait. There's plenty of time.'

They went into the bar of the Club Llueso and Alvarez ordered two coffees and two brandies.

Once they were seated, the driver said: 'What in God's name happened to the señorita?'

'I don't know much more than you do . . . Now, let's hear what happened with you.'

'It was like this. I was in the square and she comes and says she wants to go to the airport on Wednesday morning. I tell her, two thousand pesetas, she starts to beef, and we settle for eighteen hundred.

'I drive up to the house on Wednesday. 'Strewth, what a track! Like a tank obstacle course. I turn the car, open the boot, go to the front door and knock. Nothing. I knock again. Still nothing. I shout, "Señorita, we must go now or you'll miss your plane." I knock on the shutters, I do everything and it's always nothing.' He shrugged his shoulders.

The barman brought them the coffee and brandies. Alvarez poured half the brandy into his coffee, then added two spoonfuls of sugar. As he stirred, he said: 'And then?'

'What could I do but go away?'

'Naturally.'

The driver looked quickly at Alvarez, then said: 'There's one thing more. The señorita paid when she booked the taxi – said she didn't want to have many pesetas on her when she left. I tried to persuade her not to pay until the journey was made, but she insisted. Since she never went to the airport . . . What do I do with the money?'

'Forget it. A dead foreigner can't worry about eighteen hundred pesetas.'

'In that case, drink up, it's on me. And we'll have the other half as well.'

CHAPTER IX

Dr Rodriguez Roldán was a short man in his middle thirties, compactly built, with a round, rather chubby face topped by wiry black hair. His eyes were a very light blue, a strange colour for an islander. He dressed with great care, in well-cut suits, hand-made shirts, and expensive shoes. He should have looked distinguished. But for some reason, perhaps because he worked so hard at being smart, he looked slick rather than distinguished: the local kid made good and without the taste to conceal that fact.

He looked at Alvarez and said: 'From your description, she died from some kind of food poisoning.'

'That's what I'd guessed. Only it would have had to be very virulent, wouldn't it, to have prevented her calling for help?'

'She was on her own, the house hasn't a telephone, and it's a good way up the track from the next house. Perhaps she tried to ignore the symptoms at first and by the time she realized they were serious, she was in too bad a condition to leave the house to seek help.'

'A sad way to die.' He sighed. 'Anyway, the post-mortem will tell us for certain.' He was surprised that although Roldán had obviously initially been shocked by the news, he had shown little sympathy: a doctor should surely know sympathy for all his patients? 'I need to find out what kind of a man Señor Heron was – you can tell me that, can't you?'

Roldán adjusted the tooled leather blotter which was immediately in front of him on his large, ornately inlaid desk. 'Why should I be able to answer you? I was his doctor, not his personal friend.'

'You'll have gained some sort of impression.'

'Only as to his medical state. And as to his ridiculous stubbornness.' He examined his nails, then opened the left-hand top drawer of his desk and took out a small pad and briefly polished the nails of his right hand with quick, precise movements. 'He was a very sick man who should never have come out to the island.'

'What exactly was wrong with him?'

'Put as simply as possible, mitral stenosis subsequent to a bad attack of rheumatic fever when young. This was quite serious, and then on top of that he contracted a bacterial endocarditis, which is the condition in which he was when I first treated him. Surgery would probably have relieved the primary complaint, but he said he had a horror of operations and had always refused to undergo one. Then the bacterial endocarditis made it impossible for an operation to be performed, even had he been willing. My immediate advice, put very strongly, was that he should consult a specialist in Palma, but he refused. I treated him with antibiotics, but although I kept changing them he failed to respond. I again said it was essential he went into a clinic for treatment, again he refused.' Roldán replaced the nail pad in the drawer and shut this. 'There are some patients, Inspector, for whom one can do very little, thanks to their characters.'

'Did you speak to the señorita about persuading him to go into a clinic?'

'I don't see what any of this has to do with the death of the señorita?'

'Please bear with me a bit longer.'

'Very well. I told the señorita that the señor was a seriously ill man and it was more than ever essential he went into a clinic for treatment. She said she'd do what she could to persuade him, but she was no more successful than I had been.'

'How did you find her – eager to help?'

'Of course. Why shouldn't she have been?'

'There seems to have been a possibility that she was rather too friendly with another man. Did you ever get any suggestion of that?'

'No. Furthermore, I am not in the habit of listening to poisonous gossip.'

'Then there has been such gossip?'

'I was not inferring that.'

'Do you think that she looked after the señor as well as she could?'

'I think your questions are becoming not only unnecessary, but offensive.'

'I'm sorry, doctor. What finally finished off the señor?'

'It is inaccurate to suggest that anything "finally" was responsible for his death, unless he developed a sudden allergy to the latest antibiotic I tried. The course of his illness, without there being surgery, had inevitably to lead to his death. It is possible, too, that his state of emotional excitability not long before his death played some part: I have always been of the opinion that a patient's mental condition plays a far greater part in his physical condition than many fellow doctors will admit.'

'What did he get emotionally excited about?'

'The señorita told me he'd had a very heated argument over the telephone with the firm they hired their car from.'

'Which firm was it?'

'I've no idea . . . Now, if you'll excuse me, I have a number of patients I must visit.'

The surgery was in the doctor's house and as Alvarez stepped out into the hall a woman entered from the road.

In her early twenties, she had an oval face of unusual, striking beauty, framed by curly hair the colour of newly ripened corn, which suggested at one and the same time the contradictory characteristics of virginity and wantonness. Her eyes were cobalt blue and warmly emotional, yet there was also a hint of recklessness in them: her full lips were curved for smiling passion. Ye gods! he thought, if ever there'd been a woman to make any man feel that here was a citadel to be stormed for the rich rewards concealed within . . .

She studied him, accepted his obvious admiration with amusement, and walked past. He tried to persuade himself that he was far too mature to lust after a woman of her age, however exciting she might be, but he could not stop himself watching her walking towards a door and visualizing the honey-smooth, melon-sweet limbs momentarily and intriguingly outlined beneath the frock. She went through the doorway and shut the door. No wonder Francisca had been critical of her: she'd incur the resentful jealousy of every woman who saw her. Feeling suddenly old, he turned and crossed to the front door.

CHAPTER X

The manager of the car hire firm sat inside the very small office. He spread out his hands and on his wide, Mongolian face, there was an expression of surprise. 'Sure Señor Heron phoned me. So what?'

'So how was he?' asked Alvarez. 'Calm and collected?'

'You've got to be joking. He was mad: quite mad.'

There was a clanging row as a mechanic who was working on a very battered Seat 600 knocked over something. Alvarez waited until there was relative quiet before he asked: 'What had got into him?'

'He was being unreasonable, like all the foreigners. Look, I hired the señorita a car. For months it runs OK, then it breaks down. Any car can break down: yours can, mine can. I get a fresh one to her and because I strain myself to try to do too much for the customers, that also breaks down.' He gestured with his large, powerful hands. 'Any car can break down . . .'

'I got the message the first time. He bawled you out for lousy cars, eh?'

The manager used a tooth-pick to work on his teeth. After a while he turned his head and spat on to the floor. 'It was the petrol.'

'What about the petrol?'

The manager sighed. 'When I hire a car out, the tank is full. When the client brings the car back, I charge for the petrol used if the tank hasn't been refilled. The señorita had told the señor the tank of the car was over three-quarters full when it broke down.'

'And you said it was only half full and charged accordingly.'

'How d'you know that?'

'I've been around a long time.'

'Too bloody long.'

'I take it he called you a liar?'

'Foreigners have no manners. Why get excited over a few pesetas?'

'Did you know that the señor died soon after having that row with you?'

'No.'

'The doctor thinks the row might have affected him.'

'It wasn't anything to do with me: he had the row, not me.'

Alvarez jerked himself upright. 'Know something – if I were you, I'd buy some new petrol gauges. Then maybe you wouldn't meet these embarrassing situations which can so upset people.'

'I don't get embarrassed.'

Alvarez left and drove down to the harbour. He parked along the western arm and walked slowly along, studying the yachts and motor cruisers. For him, as surely for most people, a yacht epitomized wealth. A yacht gave a man command, independence, the ability to escape from it all. He sighed. Snow would drift in the Sahara before he ever owned so much as a dinghy. In any case, a man should understand the priorities. Any one of the large yachts tied up must represent something over seventy thousand square metres of prime farming land. That or a yacht? Only a fool could hesitate.

He drove back to Llueso, turning off on to the Festona Valley road, which twisted its way through small, intensely cultivated fields and past fincas, so often now in the hands of foreigners. Nearer to the mouth of the valley the road was bordered by a water channel which brought water down from a spring in the mountains to the estanquis on the farms below. The Romans had reputedly first built this aqueduct, to take the water right across to Playa Neuva, where they had maintained a garrison.

He turned left on to a very rough dirt track which made his ancient Seat creak alarmingly. The track sloped down to a ford, now dry, then climbed up through typical maquis scrub to end at wrought-iron gates. He climbed out of the car. The air was heady with the scent drawn out by the hot sun from the wild herb bushes which grew around here in such confusion.

A wide path curved round to his right, hugging the contours of the hill. The sloping land was thick with outcrops of rock and considerable imagination and labour had been used to turn the whole area into a very large rock garden, growing not only cacti and flowering bushes, but also mimosa, orange, and lemon trees. The path made a final sharp turn and then debouched on to a flat, concreted area on which was built a large bungalow. Twenty feet below the patio of the bungalow was a wide terrace in which was a swimming pool and beyond that the land, again terraced, sloped downwards, leaving a view over a belt of scrubland to the bay. He stood and stared at the scene, marvelling that despite all the years he had lived in Llueso he'd had no idea that this place existed.

'I spend a lot of my time sitting out here,' said a woman. 'It's the most beautiful view I've ever seen.'

He swung round, surprised because he had not heard her approach.

'My husband bought the land twenty years ago this month. We had nearly ten wonderful years together here before he died. He wanted to be buried up on the hillside, overlooking the garden, but although I tried very hard I couldn't get permission. But I like to think that his shade sits up there on lovely days and looks out with me.'

He knew an immediate sympathy with this slim, elderly woman who clearly cared more for practicalities than fashion and who was dressed in a faded blouse and a pair of darned, puce jeans which were much too large for her. 'If I were he, señora, I'd spend every day up there. Even when it does rain it can be so beautiful, but in a different way.'

'How right you are! Yet so many of the people out here moan that when it rains this island becomes impossibly dreary. I tell 'em, it's their minds that are dreary, not the country . . . Well, now we know we think alike on at least one subject, tell me who you are and what you want. And we might as well sit while you're doing it.'

They sat near the edge of the patio. A small boy in a swimming costume suddenly ran into view and dived into the pool, raising a fountain of spray. He swam to the far end with more enthusiasm than technique.

'That's the gardener's son,' she said, as if asked the question. 'A limb of Satan, thank God. I can't stand little boys who behave themselves: it's far too unnatural.' She turned and studied Alvarez for a while, then said: 'I've seen you about the town more than once.'

He introduced himself.

'A detective! I suppose you're here because of Betty Stevenage's death?'

'Yes, señora.'

'So a rumour's true, for once – she didn't die a natural death?'

'At the moment, nobody knows. So now I just try to find out how a woman could come to so sad an end on her own. I am told that you knew the señorita well. Is that so?'

'It's a typical exaggeration.' She began to massage her cheeks, using the tips of her fingers and rubbing in a clockwise direction. 'I'm a busybody: interested in everybody else's business. And if I can help someone, I try to do so. I kept thinking I could help Betty.'

'Why did you think that?'

'Because I was so certain she was an unhappy woman, even though when I said that to her she shouted at me to mind my own business.' She laughed. 'One of the occupational hazards of being a busybody do-gooder.'

'Why did you think she was unhappy?'

'At first I naturally reckoned it was because Bill was so ill. I told her, make him go into a clinic in Palma: there are specialists there every bit as good as the ones in England.'

'But I understand he refused to go?'

'Men can be so stupidly stubborn if you don't handle them properly. She never struck me as a woman of finesse.'

'You said this was your first thought. What was your second thought, señora?'

She stopped massaging her cheek and stared challengingly at him. 'Are you sure that any of this really matters?'

'It may matter a great deal.'

'Well, I suppose . . . I've more than half an idea that she was upset because she'd become mixed up with another man.'

'You have a reason for thinking that?'

'Yes, I have. I called at Ca'n Ibore one afternoon to see if there was any way in which I could help her. She didn't know I was coming, of course, and obviously hadn't been expecting any callers . . .' She became silent.

'Please continue, señora.'

'I went into the house and called out. No one answered so I called again. I thought I heard whispering and then she came out of one of the downstairs bedrooms. Her dress was partly undone.'

'Perhaps she had been having a siesta?'

'You're forgetting the whispering. In any case there were her eyes. A woman who has just woken up has sleepy eyes: a woman who has just made love has satiated eyes.'

'And hers were satiated?'

'Yes. And what made it all so awful was that Bill was far too ill to have been the man. Quite frankly, I was very upset.' She paused, then said crisply: 'You don't seem at all surprised?'

'I have already heard the same suggestion from someone else . . . Can you tell me who the man was?'

'I've no idea. I saw no one, and apart from the whispering, heard no one.'

'But perhaps other people have suggested a name?'

'As far as I know, no one else has the slightest idea of what has possibly been happening. I am a busybody but not, I hope, a malicious gossip.'

'Can you give me the names of men she was friendly with, even if there has been no suggestion of anything more than friendship?'

She did not answer.

'Señora, please . . .'

'I hate this.'

'I also, but as it is my job I have to do it. I promise you that I will be most discreet.'

She said: 'I'm sure you will. I often saw her with Harry Waynton. It seemed to me an unlikely relationship because they were so different in character, but then human relationships aren't founded on logic, thank God.'

'And was there anyone else?'

'No one. Betty was the kind of person who would always be lonely, even in a crowd.'

'Thank you for telling me all that you have, señora.

You've been most kind.'

'To whom?'

Down below the gardener's son tried to do a somersault off the edge of the pool and created a minor tidal wave.

During the season, the beaches became crowded to the point of discomfort. But for the few who were lucky enough to know about them, there remained small, hidden coves which offered lonely, unspoiled beauty.

Cala Tellai lay in a valley at the end of a winding dirt track four kilometres long. The rocky hills, bearing some scrub grass and a few pine trees, stretched out to sea to form a cove in which the water was a deep, rich blue except very close to the pebbly shore where it was a greeny blue. There was no pollution here, except for the occasional piece of rubbish swept in from beyond the headland or the ubiquitous clags of oil: squid and octopus jetted through the water, fish flashed silver as they turned below the surface, oursins clung to rocks with malicious immobility, and above ravens and buzzards worked the thermals.

They sat a couple of hundred metres up on the side of the cove so that they looked down on the paper-smooth water. They were under the shade of a pine, but all around them was the intense sunshine. The air shrilled to the calls of countless cicadas.

'Like Naples,' said Diana, who wore the briefest of bikinis, 'this place is so beautiful that it's a case of "See Cala Tellai and die." '

Waynton grinned. 'But like the saint who sought chastity and continency, please not just yet.'

She laughed. 'There's too much realism in you for a real dreamer.'

'I've never claimed to be that. If I had to, I'd call

myself casually down-to-earth.'

'There has to be some dreamer in you or you wouldn't be out on this island.'

'Speak to my late boss and he'll tell you it's madness, not dreaming.'

'Good! I'm all for a bit of pleasant madness.' She stretched out on the towel and her right foot moved into the sun: she automatically withdrew it. 'Predictability is so terribly boring.'

'You're in luck then, since there's not much predictability to living out here. The only predictable thing is that the unpredictable will happen.'

'That's being rose-tinted about things. So many people here are every bit as predictable as they would be in outer Wimbledon. Old Wally always tells his dirty little schoolboy jokes, Max's hands forever wander, Piers is a walking calculator on how his stocks and shares have gone up or down.'

'I wasn't really thinking so specifically – much more generally. For instance, how will each person react to living here when before he came he was almost certainly convinced it was Arcadia?'

'Start becoming personal.' She turned over on to her bronzed stomach and propped herself up on her elbows so that she could look at him through her dark glasses. 'How have you reacted?'

'Like so many English, I used to imagine that living on a Mediterranean island in the hot sun, drinking, and letting the world drift by, must be man's nearest approach to the heaven of fables.'

'Didn't I say you were part dreamer?'

'And didn't I say I was casually practical? A dreamer would have gone on dreaming and staying in England so that he could never suffer disillusionment. I came out to discover how my dreams matched up to reality.'

'You're twisting things round. A dreamer pursues his dreams: the practical man doesn't because he's so certain they're false.' She relaxed, lay out at full length and closed her eyes as she rested her head on her arms. 'So how has the dreamer – or the casual practicalist – made out?'

'He's discovered that nature abhors complete perfection. If a thing appears perfect, it contains within it the seeds of imperfection. Parts of this island are Arcadia: but because they are, they are dangerous and therefore much less than Arcadia.'

'Is that very profound?'

'It's probably pretentious tripe, but blame the wine.'

She rolled on to her side. 'What is it? Are you scared that you could be drawn too tightly to this island because it can seem so perfect?'

'Yes.'

'Then it's you who is imperfect – you've admitted to a lack of self-control.'

'Better to be a coward than fall a-over-t on the banana skin of over-confidence.' He refilled their glasses with white wine, chilled from the bottle having been kept in a freezy-bag. 'I've decided I'd better start thinking of when I'm going to go back to the UK.'

'I'm sure you're right there, Harry. It doesn't matter what I've been saying, the truth is that this place isn't any good for anyone who still has enough ambition to want to be a hundred per cent alive.'

He finished his wine. 'Do you like living here?'

'I wouldn't be here if I didn't.'

'Aren't you worried about its effects on you?'

'Not really, because it's not the same for a woman. We can remain fully alive because we carry our interests around with us so much more than you men do. And in any case, when I get too fed up with meeting the same people who keep saying the same things at the same cocktail parties, I fly back to England and have a long, sybaritic wallow among the plays, concerts, operas, films, museums, art galleries – even the television there gets better and better the longer you have to watch other countries'.'

'You're lucky to be able to go back when you want.'

'Evan has always been a very generous man.'

'Is he your husband?'

'My ex. The divorce was finalized a year ago.'

'What is he like as a person?'

'Kind, thoughtful, wealthy, and very generous.'

'Then what went wrong?'

'That's a bloody silly question! Surely to God you've enough common sense not to think that all a husband needs to offer his wife to make her happy are kindliness and a limitless dress allowance? ... The marriage was a mistake, just as much mine as his. I can't live a lie so I told him how I felt. Being the man he is, he accepted my decision and told his lawyer – much against that desiccated man's advice – to give me an irrevocable settlement in lieu of maintenance.'

'So now you're rich?'

'I've more than I need, which I suppose meets most people's idea of being rich.' She suddenly sat up to face him. 'But I'm rich only as long as I remain on my own. If ever I marry again I'm handing all that money back; irrevocable or not, because if I kept it I would be back to living a lie.'

'That leaves me free to tell you something you already know, I love you. Marry me, Diana. Your standard of living will take an almighty bump ...'

'Don't step out of character and become all corny,' she

said sharply. Then she noticed his expression and she smiled. 'Haven't you realized I can be a real bitch without even trying? Look, what I was trying to say is this, I don't ever want to be poor because it's nicer being well off – love on the dole sounds hideous. But I don't need to have wardrobes full of new clothes and a mock Tudor mansion in Bagshot to be happy. I just need to live with someone I both respect and love and who loves and respects me.'

'I qualify for the last half: what about the first?'

'I'm sorry, really sorry, Harry, but I'm not certain.'

'Competition?'

'For you – no. If I had to consider just you I'd know my feelings for sure, but I've also to worry about myself.' She leaned forward and kissed him, briefly yet with tender passion. 'You see I don't want to make a second mistake. It would be so bloody painful for both of us.' Her eyes remained rather sad as she said softly: 'Just for once, give in to the sirens' song. Let yourself drift. There's no yesterday and no tomorrow, only today to be enjoyed without thought or consequence.'

CHAPTER XI

Superior Chief Salas was an impatient man and scornful of anyone whose mind appeared to work less quickly than his own. 'Don't you understand? I want to know whether the señorita did or did not die from natural causes?'

Alvarez sighed as he held the telephone receiver a little away from his ear. 'Señor, until the results of the post-mortem . . .'

'Surely you've conducted at least some sort of an investigation into the circumstances of her death?'

'Indeed I have . . .'

'Then with what results?'

'I suppose to be accurate, señor, I should say that at the moment there aren't any.'

'Why not?'

'It hasn't been easy . . .'

'I imagine you find considerable difficulty in most things.'

In many ways, that was true.

'I want a full report on the present state of the investigations on my desk first thing tomorrow morning. Is that quite clear?'

'Indeed, señor.'

Salas hardly bothered to say goodbye before ringing off. Alvarez replaced the receiver, sighed, ran the palm of his hand over his forehead at the point where the hair was receding far too quickly for his peace of mind, and sighed again. He reached down to the bottom right-hand drawer of the desk and brought out a glass and a half-full bottle of brandy.

He poured himself out a large drink and lit a cigarette. Sudden and unexpected death always raised questions, but usually these were quickly answered: the English, though, forever ungraciously awkward, seemed unable to die straightforwardly. It seemed as if Señorita Stevenage had died from some form of natural food poisoning. But wouldn't she have felt the symptoms become worse and worse, and even if she had initially ignored them have made every effort to summon help instead of remaining in the kitchen? True Ca'n Ibore was partially isolated and without a telephone, but still it was difficult to believe she could not have dragged herself to the next house . . . If she had been poisoned, surely the motive must concern her lover? Francisca had heard her tell a man that she loved him and he wasn't going to mess around with other women or she'd make trouble for him: Señora Browning had visited the house unexpectedly and had been met by a woman whose eyes betrayed the fact that she had just been making love. (It made a man uneasy to learn how far a woman's eyes betrayed her to another woman.) After the death of Señor Heron, whom she had been betraying so callously, had she expected her lover to love her openly, perhaps marry her? And had he decided that his only way of escape was to murder her, either because he didn't love her that much, or he was married and unable or unwilling to obtain a divorce . . . ?

Alvarez entered the block of flats and climbed the stairs and by the time he reached the third floor he was sweating profusely. He ate, smoked, and drank far too much: one day he would go on a diet, give up smoking, and limit himself to one drink a day.

Waynton opened the door of Flat 10. Alvarez saw a face which suggested its owner had been around, had taken and given a few hard knocks, and had learned to face the world with a wry sense of humour.

They went into the sitting-room which was also the dining-room, and sat.

'Señor,' said Alvarez, in his slow, tired-sounding voice, 'you will know that Señorita Stevenage died and that her death was unfortunately not discovered until yesterday morning. I am now having to make certain enquiries. I understand you knew the señorita well?'

'Without wishing to quibble, it depends what you mean by "well". I saw her quite often, but only casually and it was merely a case of having a drink together or even just a chat.'

'Will you tell me if you liked her?'

Waynton looked curiously at the detective. 'I suppose I didn't really think of her in those terms. She was just an acquaintance.'

'Then I wonder why, if you were not so very friendly with her, you saw her so frequently?'

'Isn't all this very immaterial?'

'It may be of importance, señor.'

'Why? Because there's something odd about her death?'

'I cannot answer you because I do not yet know.'

'But you suspect or you wouldn't be asking these questions?'

Alvarez made no comment.

'You asked me why I saw Betty as often as I did – it's because she only had to see me in the far distance to rush over and nobble me.'

'Nobble you?'

Waynton allowed his irritation to surface. 'I was introduced to her at a party and I said all the conventional, meaningless things one does and very quickly decided that we hadn't much in common. Usually if one feels like that the other person does as well, so when you meet you just smile and pass on. But she only had to see me to make a beeline over to wherever I was. It got so I became chary of sitting in the square for a drink.'

'Do you think she had become very attracted to you?'

'I knew she wasn't. Or to put it a bit more accurately, I was convinced she wasn't.'

'Then why should she have so insisted on meeting you?'

'God knows! In the end I came to the conclusion that all she really wanted was someone to talk to. She didn't get on well with most of the other residents and I suppose I gave the impression of listening sympathetically. To tell the truth, I began to feel rather guilty because if I saw her before she saw me I'd duck out of the way.'

'What would she talk about?'

Waynton shrugged his shoulders. 'Nothing much – just to add to the confusion. I'd ask her how Bill was, what the doctor had said . . . And she'd sometimes hardly bother to answer. There'd be long, unpregnant silences.'

'Did she not speak about other residents who live here?'

'I suppose so.'

'Can you remember who she mentioned?'

Waynton, reluctant to recall memories of a woman who had died so distressingly, finally said: 'I really can only remember the last time. I was in the square, waiting for Diana who was late, and Betty came to the table. She started asking who I imagined Diana was out with. She suggested two names and these were quite ridiculous because Diana couldn't stand the sight of either man.'

'Would you be kind enough to give me their names?'

'But as Diana disliked them both . . .'

'Please, señor, their names?'

'Alex Dunton and Gordon Elliott.'

'And can you tell me where they live?'

Waynton gave their addresses.

Alvarez finished writing on the back of a crumpled envelope and looked up. 'One more question, señor. Would you believe that Señorita Stevenage was a woman whose emotions would become very involved with another person other than Señor Heron?'

'I didn't know her well enough to answer you.'

Alvarez nodded, then stood. 'Thank you very much for all your help,' he said, with formal courtesy.

CHAPTER XII

Alvarez parked his car in front of a squarish bungalow set among the maquis scrub. It was an unimaginative, graceless bungalow, made no more attractive, since it was so obviously fake, by the steepled well in front of the patio.

Alex Dunton was tall and thin and he had a creased, lean face which held a raffish air that was reinforced by a golf-club secretary's moustache. He had the kind of laugh most frequently heard in the saloon bar at a favourite local and he dressed with great attention to detail and impeccable bad taste, often in country checks. Diana's nickname for him, Provincial Percy, was cruel but not inaccurate.

'Señor,' said Alvarez, as he sat down in an uncomfortable chair on the patio, 'I have to ask some questions concerned with Señorita Stevenage's death.'

'So it's true she didn't die naturally? Well, it's not much good coming here. I hardly knew the woman.'

'But I understand that you were friendly with her?'

Dunton laughed contemptuously. '*De mortuis nil nisi bonus*, and all that, but give me a bit of credit for taste.'

'Was she not rather beautiful, then?'

'Depends how you like 'em, doesn't it?'

'And how do you like them, señor?'

'That's a good question! With a bit more *je ne sais quoi* than she'd got, that's for starters.'

'Did you see her very often?'

'You've got things all wrong. I didn't see her at all unless I couldn't get out of the way quickly enough.'

'When you did see her, where would this be?'

'Where? What a damned funny question. Where d'you think? In the street, at the post office collecting the mail on the odd occasion I found the place open . . .' He shrugged his shoulders.

'Tell me, did you ever visit the señorita at Ca'n Ibore?'

'Now you're joking! Don't you understand, I couldn't stand the woman. Look, all this is a load of cod's, so let's have an end to it, right?'

'As this is a police matter, señor, regretfully you must continue to answer my questions.'

Dunton looked scornfully at Alvarez, wanting to show his contempt for the muddling stupidity of foreigners, but as always he could not prevent himself feeling uneasy in the face of authority.

'I wonder,' said Alvarez with quiet curiosity, almost as if he were really putting the question to himself, 'whether it is not the truth that you knew the señorita a little better than you wish to say?'

'For Pete's sake! I hardly knew her, I didn't like her, and I'm sorry she's dead but I'm not going to start wearing black because of it.'

'Then if all that is true, why should she have been so interested in what you were doing?'

'This is becoming even more bloody daft. She wouldn't have given a damn if I'd been living it up with a mermaid.'

'It seems that she did worry, señor. For instance, there was the day when she was very keen to know if you were seeing Señora Carrington.'

'Like hell.'

'I assure you, it was so. She became quite excited.'

'Who have you been listening to? Some of the people out here have got bloody twisted senses of humour.'

'In this case I think the person was quite serious. Do you

know Señora Carrington?'

'What if I do?'

'Perhaps you are friendly with her?'

'What are you getting at now?'

'I wish only to discover the truth.'

'Well, the truth about her doesn't take much discover-ing. She's one highly stuck-up bitch. Thinks herself no end of a *crème de la crème*, but I'm telling you she's no smarter than the next bit of bint and she's twice as scratchy.'

'Señor, are you married?'

'What's that to do with anybody else if I am?'

'And the señora lives here, with you?'

'Where the hell d'you think my wife's going to live?' He stood up. 'Señor, as you are English that is a question impossible to answer.'

Gordon Elliott lived on the north side of Llueso, in a modernized finca on a hill: from the garden, one could see both Llueso and Playa Neuva bays. He was tall and too thin for his height, so that he looked bean-poley. He might have been considered good-looking but for the signs of weakness in his face, which made him appear perpetually apologetic. By contrast his wife, who was large if not exactly fat, looked as if she hadn't ever apologized in the whole of her life.

Alvarez, as he stood in the entrance room which was also the sitting-room, explained the reason for his visit.

'A very nasty business,' said Avis, in her deep, masculine voice. 'Of course we can see why you have to check up. So ask away. And do sit down – there's no extra charge for using the chairs.'

He sat. 'Señora, I regret, but the questions are for your husband.'

'I realize that.'

'Then I think it would be best if I spoke to him on his own.'

Her manner became frosty.

'Avis, don't you think it might be best if you left,' said Elliott nervously.

'There's nothing,' she snapped, 'which you can possibly say which cannot be said in front of me.' She stood in the centre of the room, hands on hips. Alvarez smiled patiently. 'Very well! It's the kind of thing one expects from this country. I'll go into the village and do the shopping.' She left, trailing her sharp annoyance behind her.

Elliott waited until they heard a car door slam before saying: 'I'm afraid my wife gets a little impatient at times.'

'It is a woman's prerogative, señor . . . Now, if we may discuss Señorita Stevenage. She was a friend of yours?'

'Oh no, not a friend. That is, if you mean someone we knew well and liked to see a lot of.'

'But you did know her?'

They heard the car drive off. Elliott took a coloured handkerchief from his pocket and mopped his forehead. 'We knew her to speak to, of course. But nothing more than that. She didn't go out much and anyway . . . Well, my wife didn't like her. You must know what it's like when the ladies take a dislike to someone. You just can't talk them into being charitable.'

'Was it, then, necessary to become charitable?'

'I suppose that's being very unkind. But Betty was . . . Well, she was what I'd call gauche. And she did seem to resent so much and she was always being clumsily rude, if you know what I mean.'

'Did you ever visit her at Ca'n Ibore?'

'We never went there, no.'

'I mean you on your own, señor.'

Elliott stared at him in surprise. 'Good God, no!'

'Are you quite certain?'

'Of course I am.'

'Yet one day Señorita Stevenage was very concerned because she thought you might be out with Señora Carrington.'

'That . . . that's impossible.'

'It seems not. Can you say why Señorita Stevenage should have been concerned if she and you were not close friends?'

'But that's a terrible inference to make. I hardly knew her and yet you're trying to suggest . . .' He swallowed heavily.

'Do you know Señora Carrington?'

'Of course I do.'

'How well do you know her?'

'You're not going to start inferring anything more, surely to God?' He stared at the front door again. 'We just knew her to speak to, that's all. Avis never wanted to get too friendly because she says Diana's too fast. After all, she is divorced and she's always going round with different men.' He didn't realize it, but there was now a trace of wistfulness in his voice.

Alvarez was silent for a few seconds, then he said: 'Thank you for your help, señor.'

Just before Alvarez left, Elliott said urgently: 'You must believe me. I've never been out with either of the ladies. In fact, I've . . . I've never been out with anyone else but Avis since we were married.'

As Alvarez drove slowly down the narrow lane which wound round the side of the hill, he thought about the two men. Dunton was the eternal womanizer. A lot of women would be attracted by his raffish, slap-and-tickle character and he wouldn't think twice about betraying his wife.

Elliott would think a hundred and one times about actually betraying his wife and even to look lustfully at another woman would fill him with worry for fear his wife might find out. But his weakness could provide a challenge to some women and if the challenge were strong enough, Elliott would surely succumb to their blandishments?

CHAPTER XIII

Down in the Port, Diana drove along the front to a parking space, then left her car and walked along what had now become a path, closed to traffic, until she came to the jetty from which ski boats were allowed to take off. She saw Waynton in the water beyond the pier giving instructions to a young man. She sat on a bollard and when an ice-cream tricycle came along and stopped she bought a strawberry cone.

The ski boat's engine started and settled down into a regular rhythm. Waynton gave the signal and the helmsman took up the slack in the ski lines and then knifed the boat through the water. The two skiers came upright and for a short while cut parallel lines through the water. Then the tyro began to lose his balance, tried frantically to regain it but inevitably was flipped over in a flurry of spray. Waynton released his tow bar and sank gracefully down into the water. The ski boat, revs down, circled round.

After a short while the skiers tried again. Waynton was at ease, the other man was clumsy but gaining confidence as he managed to stay upright. They raced across the bay towards the distant shore, fuzzy because of the heat haze.

She finished the cone, pushing some of the ice-cream down with her tongue as she had done ever since a child, so that the last mouthful was not solely one of biscuit. She lit a cigarette. She could, she thought, so easily have said 'Yes' in Cala Tellai. What more did she need to know about Harry's feelings for her, or her feelings for him? To put the question was to know the answer. The memory of

Evan and the sad bitterness of a marriage which had started, as all marriages should, in a cloud of excitement and had then deteriorated into dull unhappiness. Evan, she'd discovered only after their marriage, needed to be dominated, not physically but mentally. The facile explanation for this would probably be that it was because his father had died when he'd been very young and his mother had brought him up far more strictly than could possibly have been necessary: but Diana was fairly certain he'd have wanted to be dominated however he'd been brought up.

She'd been amused when, on their honeymoon, he'd kept deferring to her wishes and her opinions and apologizing for his own. That was love. But then she'd discovered, as time lengthened, that it wasn't love, it was an emotional masochism (for want of a more accurate description) and she had sadly come to despise him because in her eyes he had become less than a man. And because she had to respect to love, she had ceased to love him: to cease to love him meant she could no longer live with him. He had begged and begged her to stay. She suspected that the marriage had become even more precious to him when he knew that she no longer loved but despised him. In the end, realizing that she would never alter her decision, he had characteristically insisted on settling a large capital sum on her and making this settlement irrevocable. The grand gesture of an honourable, if weak, man? Or a masochistic gesture?

Harry was not like Evan. And yet had Evan been like Evan before the marriage? It was a Catch 22 situation. Never marry a man until you can be certain what his character is: you can never be certain of a man's character until you've married him.

She left her thoughts and returned to the present. The

ski boat was pounding its way back across the bay, taking a broad sweep towards the headlands to keep clear of a large ketch. She saw that there was only one skier now, Harry, because the other man was a passenger in the boat. He was sweeping from side to side, riding over the wake with inclined body and at each turn sending up sheets of curling spray. He made it look like a ballet on water.

Close to the pier the boat slowed and turned and Waynton let go of the rope. He slowly, gracefully, subsided into the water.

He gave the boat owner a hand to secure and it was twenty minutes before he came up to where she sat. 'Hi! I wish I'd known before that you were here – I'd have got Dick to give you a run on the skis.'

'It's just as well you didn't. He and I are agreed that we heartily dislike each other.'

'Why so?'

'He's a fool.'

He laughed. 'Now tell me what's got you extra sharp and scratchy?'

'I've a head.'

'Then I can't think of a more sensible way of dealing with that than sitting out in the blazing sunshine.'

She slid off the bollard and linked her arm with his. 'It's nice to discover you're the sympathetic type. Harry, I'd like a coffee.'

'I'll pick up my clobber and we'll go to the café further along.'

They walked past large houses, hedged in with palms for the shade and walls often ablaze with bougainvillaea, and came to a café which fronted the beach.

As soon as they were seated and he had ordered, he said: 'Is something wrong?'

She didn't immediately answer, but opened her handbag and brought out a slim gold cigarette case and offered it.

'I hope if there is, it's nothing serious?' He struck a match for her.

'There is trouble, but it's nothing to do with me. It's to do with you.'

'As far as I know I'm as trouble-free as the wind.'

'Do you know Avis Elliott?'

'By sight – which is as familiar as I want to get with her.'

'She's going round the place saying that Betty was murdered and probably you murdered her.'

He stared at her in amazement, then laughed.

'Don't be so bloody stupid,' she snapped exasperatedly.

'Me stupid? I'm obviously not in the same league as dear Avis.'

'Why won't you take anything seriously?'

'Because most things don't deserve to be. That woman is responsible for more nonsense talked than half a dozen other females all put together. But let's be charitable. If you're married to a man like Gordon, you've got to find something to do to stop yourself going crazy.'

'Haven't you the wit to realize that a lot of people listen to what she says.'

'All right. So there are a few simple souls who'll give themselves a thrill by believing her. So what?'

She shook her head in a gesture of impatient annoyance. Before she could say anything, though, the waiter brought two cups of coffee to their table.

She slit open a small pack of sugar and poured half of this into her cup. As she stirred slowly, she looked at him and said: 'Suppose Betty didn't die accidentally?'

'Why suppose any such thing? If Avis said she didn't, it's ten to one she did.'

'But there hasn't been a funeral yet because they're carrying out a post-mortem.'

'It's probably the same here as at home – if a death's sudden and unexpected, there's a PM as a pure matter of course.'

'But apparently there's been a detective around, asking people a lot of questions.'

'Right. He's been to my place, asked his questions, and got his answers. It doesn't signify anything.'

'Of course it does. Detectives don't go around asking people personal questions unless they've a reason to. Did he want to know if you were friendly with Betty and had visited her at her house?'

'Yes.'

'Harry, why d'you suppose this detective is asking those particular questions?'

'I can only imagine that if there is a hint of something wrong they believe that maybe she'd been messing around with a bloke while Bill was confined to his bed.'

'And who's the only person known to have been at all friendly with her? You.'

'Which by devious routes leads to today's bad joke. Is that Avis's line of reasoning? If so, she needs to fumigate her mind. I felt sorry for Betty, but as for bedding her while Bill was slowly pegging out upstairs . . .'

'The gossips of the town are going to have a field day.'

'Then the best of British imperial luck to them!'

The sunshine edged past the outermost branches of a pine tree to fall directly on her face and she opened her handbag and brought out a pair of dark spectacles. 'Don't take this lightly, Harry. Things could easily get unpleasant for you.'

'Things'll get more unpleasant for anyone who comes and accuses me.'

'There won't be any direct accusations. There'll be whispers and then more whispers. It's a tight little community here, so if it got bad life could become rather impossible for you.' She fiddled with the cigarette, twisting it round between forefinger and thumb, then suddenly stubbing it out. Without looking up, she said: 'You were talking about its being time to leave the island and return to the UK. Why not speed things up and go quickly? That way, you'd pull the rug from under their feet.'

He showed his amazement. 'You're suggesting I cut and run away with my tail between my legs because a tired old gossip is naming me as a candidate for a murder that almost certainly never was?'

'You're not running away as you've done nothing to run away from. You'd just be easing yourself out of an unpleasant situation that was none of your making. If only you could recognize such a thing, you'd know that that was common sense.'

He laughed. 'Ten out of ten for semantic ingenuity, nought out of ten for logic.'

'Damn you, I was only trying to help,' she snapped.

He managed to sound chastened. 'I'm terribly sorry and I humbly apologize.'

'Liar.'

He reached across the table and put his hand on hers. 'This is genuine. Thanks for your reasons . . . The real trouble is I was born stubborn and I've just gone on developing.'

'So instead of being sensible and leaving, you're going to stay and stick your solid head out for everyone to stamp on?' She sat back, annoyed and exasperated . . . And yet also glad.

*

Alvarez sat under the shade of an olive tree whose massive, gnarled, twisted trunk seemed to speak of some past agony, and stared out across the fields. Tomatoes, peppers, aubergines, lettuces, beans, potatoes, groundnuts, plums, apricots, almonds, walnuts, pomegranates, figs, oranges, lemons ... Man would never have lost his soul if only he had stayed close to the soil.

He sighed, reached over and picked up the last piece of bread which had been coated with olive oil and sprinkled with salt. The sun was dipping down towards the mountain tops, highlighting their crests. Time to return to the office. Soon, he thought miserably, the phone in the office was going to ring and Superior Chief Salas would impatiently be demanding to know what was happening in the case of the dead Englishwoman. Well, what was happening? She had died an unpleasant death: why? She had probably had a lover who had usurped her other, dying lover: who?

He ate the bread and lit a cigarette. The señorita had not eaten mussels for lunch on that last day, so why had there been mussel shells and a segment of lemon in the bucket under the sink? Had she eaten some mussels before sitting down at the table where she had eaten more? Why eat some in the kitchen and the rest at the table? ... Had two people eaten mussels, had one been taken fatally ill, and had the other tried to hide all traces of his visit but in the stress of the moment had acted instinctively and before washing up his plates and cutlery swept the shells into the waste bucket under the sink?

The short, fat man who stood at the bar of the restaurant between Llueso and the Port tapped the side of his nose several times. 'You mark my words, there's something very funny about Betty's death.'

The other man present momentarily looked up from his sixth gin and tonic. 'Funny ha-ha or funny peculiar – makes a big difference, you know?'

'Funny ve-rey peculiar. There's been a detective going around asking questions.'

He finished his drink. 'Bert,' he shouted. 'Hurry up. My throat's like bloody sandpaper.'

'Alex said this detective asked him how well he knew Betty and had he ever visited her house on the q.t.'

'Had he?'

'Apparently not.'

'Pity.'

The bartender finally appeared through the doorway behind the bar.

'Heard the latest, Bert? Mr Cochrane's just told me that that young filly was murdered.'

'You don't say, sir!'

'I didn't say,' snapped the short, fat man irritably. 'But it does look as if her death can't have been accidental.'

'Can't see the difference myself: too subtle. Trouble with the world today – it's all become too subtle . . . Now am I going to get that drink?'

CHAPTER XIV

On the Friday, and for the first time in over two weeks, the sky was cloudy at daybreak. But by midday few clouds were left and these, drifting in front of a light westerly wind, cast no more than temporary shadows on the land below.

The restaurant was sited dramatically, poised a hundred and fifty metres above the rock-strewn sea with its balcony stretching out beyond the cliff edge. In the evening diners could watch the sun sink below the horizon, flooding sea and sky with an infinity of reds and oranges.

Compton ordered wine and the wine waiter left. 'As I never tire of saying, this is one of the few restaurants on the island to know what service really means.'

'Why the enthusiasm?' asked Diana. 'Because they call you "sir"?'

He smiled. 'As needle sharp as ever and twice as piercing! It's because the tables are laid with clean table-cloths and silver, the waiters know which is the correct side, and the food is served, not slapped down with a take-it or leave-it attitude.'

'If the food's good what's it matter whether it's served on your right or your wrong side?'

'There are times when it makes a subtle difference to one's enjoyment of it.'

'Only if you're being pompous.'

'You're not going to convince me that there aren't moments when you of all people don't prefer eating in style.'

'If I want servility I don't look for it on this island. The people aren't servile, thank God!'

The waiter brought them their drinks: she had a Campari and sweet vermouth, he had a gin and tonic.

'Cheers.' He smiled. 'Even if it's now considered very LMC to say "cheers".'

'Christ, those labels! Where d'you live, what school did you go to, is it true your aunt's cousin's nephew is titled? Why can't we English accept each other for what we actually are and not for our backgrounds?'

'But what are we?'

'Right now I expect you'd name me bitch and yourself long-suffering.'

'I hope I'd be slightly more subtle than that.'

'I'm sure you would be. Nothing too, too direct for Hugh Compton, noted democratic bon viveur.'

He laughed. 'All right, that's me tabbed and tabulated ... By the way, I've just had a letter from a friend of mine who lives near Cannes. He's got rather a nice place up in the hills.'

'Would any friend of yours live in a hovel?'

'To listen to them, some of them do ... This house is an old one, recently modernized, and when it was being used as a farmhouse Renoir painted it. Jocelyn wanted to buy that painting – until it came up for sale and made as many thousands as he could have afforded tens.'

'What's supposed to be the moral of that story?'

'No moral. Just a snippet of information which might have been received with interest but wasn't.'

She smiled, for the first time that evening. 'All right, in your ever-so-charming way you've indicated I'm not being good company.'

He studied her. 'Obviously something's worrying you?'

She nodded.

'There's a saying which no doubt you'd dismiss with

scorn: a trouble shared is a trouble halved.'

'Out here a trouble shared is a trouble published . . . There's no secret. I'm worried about Harry. You must have heard what people are saying?'

He drank, replaced the glass on the table, and idly traced a pattern across the frosting with his forefinger. 'You mean about Betty? I've heard one or two nonsenses, but I didn't give them ear-room. No one will pay any attention to them.'

'Some people are. Why can't they see . . .' She stopped.

'See what?'

'That because of the kind of person he is he'd never hurt a woman, whatever happened. As for doing anything so filthy as poisoning her . . .'

'Is it now certain, then, that she was poisoned?'

'Nothing out here is ever certain.'

Compton traced another pattern on his glass. He said, somewhat hesitantly: 'Do you know just how friendly he was with her?'

'He was sorry for her and offered her a sympathetic ear and as no one else would do that she'd always make a beeline for him whenever she saw him. That's all there was to the friendship . . . Which people are now trying to make out was red hot.'

'Perhaps she thought there was more to it than he did?'

'Of course she didn't.'

'Sometimes women do get fixations.'

'Not nearly as often as men would like to think. He never went to the house.'

'According to the rumours, though, someone must have done. She was heard there with a man and it was pretty obvious that they weren't just good friends.'

'These bloody rumours.'

'This one may have a little more substance to it than

usual. The maid who worked for Betty and Bill is said to
have heard what was going on. There'd be no reason for
her to make up gossip, would there?'

'She probably didn't hear a thing and the whole story is
just a load of cod's. In any case, what if Betty was messing
around with another man?'

He looked curiously at her.

'Well?'

'Suppose Betty was poisoned – who poisoned her? The
murderer would have had to have a very strong motive
and that surely means knowing her well. The man at the
house, if there was such a man, must have known her
well.'

'And because Harry was sometimes seen with her in
town he has to be that man?'

'That's the way people are talking.'

'God, you can't get stupider than that.' Just because
Harry had been friendly with her . . . Other men must
have known her, far better than Harry . . . Yet in a small
community where everyone knew everyone, why was it no
one could suggest another name?

The waiter brought them their first course and they ate.
Compton, with quiet tact, turned the conversation away
from Betty and Harry Waynton and soon had her laugh-
ing at one of his droller stories.

They returned to Llueso over the mountain road, often
dramatically and starkly beautiful, and they were passing
above Laraix monastery, encircled by mountains, when
he said: 'You know I mentioned Jocelyn's place in Cannes
earlier on? I thought I'd go and stay with him later, maybe
nearer the autumn. I've always had a yen to live in the
south of France. How about coming over sometimes and
joining us there?'

'I don't know.'

'It would be great for me and it would let you escape from the rather claustrophobic atmosphere of this place.'

She didn't answer. Harry, she kept assuring herself, couldn't have done such a vile thing. And yet each time she told herself this, the thought floated through her mind that Betty had had a lover and no one else was known to have been friendly with her.

CHAPTER XV

The phone rang at twenty minutes past eleven on Saturday morning and Alvarez, grunting from the effort, reached over and lifted the receiver.

'You remember the Cifret case?' said Superior Chief Salas. It was more a directive than a question. 'He is reported to be in England – the police there have been on to us through Interpol. We've no prints for a definite identification so as you know him by sight you're to go over and, if necessary, arrange for extradition.'

'Do what, señor?' asked Alvarez, misbelieving his senses.

'You're booked on this afternoon's flight. There'll be a man at the airport at fourteen hundred hours to give you your ticket, the file on the case, and our official request for extradition. Detective-Inspector Fletcher will be arranging for you to be met at Heathrow airport and driven down to Bearstone.'

'Señor, surely there is someone else . . .'

'While I'm on to you, I can tell you that the post-mortem conducted on Señorita Stevenage has been concluded. No trace of organic, inorganic, or vegetable poison was discovered in her body so death is assumed to have been caused by ordinary food poisoning. In view of the contents of her stomach and of your preliminary report this is named as mytilotoxin. I am assured that because of the advanced state of decomposition it is quite impossible to be more specific. There will, of course, have to be an investigation into the source of the mussels she ate, but that will not directly concern us. Is everything clear? Goodbye.'

He slowly replaced the receiver. Mother of God, England! Fog, rain, snow, ice: people of frozen emotions . . . He poured himself out a very large brandy.

Some considerable time passed before his thoughts became sufficiently calm for him to consider the rest of the message. Señorita Stevenage had not been poisoned, she had died a natural death from food poisoning: taken ill, she had waited too long before trying to summon aid and then, because of the isolated position of the house, she had tragically discovered she had left it too late. That she had had a lover even while a former lover lay dying upstairs was of no account except to her immortal soul. And since she had been English, she would never have considered that.

London had frightened him, not because of the size since he had expected a vast city, but because of the cold in-humanity of the endless streets of tight-packed grey houses. A man could be born, live, and die, among such sur-roundings and never know what colour meant.

As they had driven southwards and left behind them those millions of prisoners, they had passed through countryside. He had stared at the fields with amazement. Not even when it rained for a week on end on the island did the fields grow so lushly green. And the trees. Huge chestnuts, ashes, oaks and beeches, which spread majesti-cally upwards and outwards, almost without end. And the fat sleek cattle in herds so large it was difficult to believe each herd belonged to only one farm.

Throughout the journey the driver, a sergeant, had talked about Mallorca. Three years before, he and his family had spent a fortnight on the island, he didn't know where but it had been great. Grand hotel, cheap booze, plenty of other couples to drink and dance with, and sun from dawn to dusk just like the travel posters had promised. Proudly, Alvarez had tried to explain that the coastal concrete jungles were totally unrepresentative of the island, so beautiful where man had not betrayed his heritage in the pursuit of money, but sadly he'd discovered that the sergeant wasn't interested in the natural beauties: on holidays he wanted sand, sun, and cheap booze.

Bearstone proved to be a large market town, its previous character all but obliterated by development. It was ringed by low-cost housing and as they drove through the streets of semi-detacheds Alvarez once more felt a chill settle on him. Perhaps hell was not really a place of fire and brimstone, but of grey houses, all alike, under a leaden sky.

County police headquarters was a large, pseudo-Georgian building, with an imposing entrance hall and grand staircase up to the first floor. Above the first floor, however, the staircases were very ordinary and the corridors were uncarpeted. The sergeant led him along to an end room on the third floor. It was not a large room, yet two desks had been packed into it, together with a glass-fronted bookcase, a battered coat-stand, and two tall filing cabinets.

'I'm Detective-Inspector Fletcher: Tom Fletcher,' said the only man present, who had been seated behind the left-hand desk. He came forward and shook hands.

Alvarez saw a tall, broad-shouldered, slim-waisted man who looked as if his suit had been ironed on to him only half an hour before. He was masculinely yet smoothly handsome and obviously completely self-assured, the kind of combination demanded by the importers of the better Havana cigars for their TV commercials.

'Glad to see you. Do grab a seat. I'm sure you'd like some coffee.' He turned and spoke to the sergeant, his voice now a shade more clipped. 'Organize two cups, will you please, Breeden. And get them from the canteen, not that vending machine which makes everything taste so peculiar.'

As Alvarez sat he gloomily reflected on the fact that he had not been asked if he would like some coffee, it had just been assumed that he would. Men of the stamp of this detective-inspector were always so very quick to assume.

Fletcher, his movements crisply economical, sat down behind his desk. 'Did you have a good trip over?'

'Yes, thank you, señor.' He was about to talk about the journey when the D.I. spoke again.

'Good . . . Now, you won't want to waste time so let's get down to business. You'll go along to the prison tomorrow morning and interview the man on remand to see if he is Cifret. We're holding him on one charge, but I gather that if you do identify him you'll ask for extradition on a far more serious one. I presume you've brought the usual T three-one-six form?'

Alvarez tried to sort out his muddled thoughts. 'The what form, señor?'

Fletcher's eyebrows rose fractionally, but otherwise he had the manners not to show his astonishment. 'You did not – ' He paused, as if having trouble in finding the exact words he wished to use – 'glance through your paperwork before leaving?'

'There was no time. All the papers were only given to me at the airport.'

Fletcher nodded, but it was impossible to believe that he would have boarded the plane before satisfying himself that all necessary papers were tabulated and indexed. 'Then we will have to make certain in a moment that everything's in order. The courts can become very sticky over ridiculous procedural questions.' He picked up a sheet of foolscap paper and briefly looked down at it. 'I've had an itinerary drawn up for you – perhaps you'd care to glance through it?'

Alvarez tried to rise, but first he had to uncross his legs and by the time he'd done this – his right shoe caught in some part of the chair – Fletcher was round the side of the desk and handing him the paper. He read. Provisional time of arrival at county HQ – he was delighted to discover they'd been a few minutes out – provisional time of departure to The Round Tower Hotel where he would occupy room no. 61, evening meal served between seven and nine. Sunday 25 June police car to arrive at hotel at 0900 hours, proceeding to Bearstone Central Jail where prisoner Rodolfo Zamora (as he claimed he was named) to be interviewed. Monday 26 June, provisional time for consultation with legal experts on subject of application for extradition ... Mother of God, was life itself timed and dated to the last second?

Fletcher looked at his watch. 'I'm afraid that I have to leave in five minutes, but Detective-Sergeant Wraight will be coming in and he'll drive you to your hotel. Incidentally, he's in charge of the evening's entertainment.'

'Entertainment, señor?'

'There's a very popular film on which I'm sure you'll like and provided you have a quick dinner you'll be in time to make the last showing.'

Alvarez longed to explain that he was tired and mentally worn out and that he liked to take his time over dinner, so he'd really rather not go anywhere, but he funked telling the D.I. that he wanted to disturb the so carefully prepared itinerary.

CHAPTER XVI

The McKays were American and rich and, unusually, they lived the kind of social democracy their nation so often preached. People who accepted their invitations could never be certain whom they were going to meet, but since their parties were justly famous most people were willing to risk the hazards.

It was after nine when Waynton arrived at Ca Na Chunga. He pulled his Mobylette up on its stand and then went round the side of the house to the large covered patio and the swimming pool. After a quick check he saw Diana on the far side of the pool. She was talking to Jessica Appleton.

'I'm hell's bells late,' he said, as soon as he reached Diana. 'Couldn't get the Mobylette to go. Tried everything from cleaning the plug to draining the carburettor and in the end I suffered a wild anger and kicked the flywheel. Started like a bird after that.' He half turned. 'How's life with you, Jessica?'

Jessica had, not without reason, been compared to a hoopoe: her face was long and beaky, her dresses were often extravagantly coloured and she liked ruffled hats, and she was always bobbing her head. She looked at Waynton with a sharp interest which she made no effort to hide. 'I'm surprised to see you here . . .'

Diana interrupted her. 'Harry, have you got a fag on you? I meant to buy some at the bar and clean forgot when I came past.'

He offered her a pack.

'You ought to stop smoking,' said Jessica, who had

decided opinions on everything. 'Daddy never smoked in all his life and he lived to be eighty-two.'

'And my grandfather smoked umpteen cigars a day and lived to be ninety,' snapped Diana. She flicked open her lighter.

'Cigars are different. They're gentlemanly . . . I didn't expect to see you here, Harry.' She tilted her head to one side.

Diana said: 'Simone told me the Youngers have come back. Is that right?'

'They came back at the end of last week and are renting a really awful place at seventeen thousand a month. I told them, seventeen thousand for that kind of a place is quite ridiculous and it only leads the Mallorquins on to asking stupider and stupider rents from other people. Harry, have you . . .'

'Someone said the new people have moved into the Hannas' house,' interrupted Diana. 'They're supposed to be rather pleasant and she paints.'

'Perhaps she sells to chocolate-box manufacturers . . . Harry, is it true they've confiscated your passport?'

A maid came round with glasses and a bottle of champagne, wrapped in a napkin, and Diana and Jessica had their glasses refilled and Waynton was given a glass newly filled.

'When I was trying to get the Mobylette to start,' said Waynton, 'I nearly went mad from visions of chilled champagne.'

'Daddy always called it a ladies' drink.' Jessica turned. 'Harry, what's happened to your passport?'

'I'm sorry to disappoint you, but I've still got it.'

'D'you mean that the detective didn't take it away?'

'That's right. He came to my place and asked a few questions, then left, empty-handed. No passport confiscated, no handcuffs, no early morning meeting with a garotte.'

'But he did ask you a lot of questions?'

'As I've just said.'

'Why did he ask them?'

'Because someone had told him I used to be friendly with Betty. When I assured him the friendship had been highly platonic, he left.'

She studied him, plainly disappointed. Then she looked past his right shoulder. 'There's Pauline. Mary says she's had a terrible row with the Maddons. She is *so* hot-tempered, especially when she's had one or two too many drinks.' She suddenly darted off, pushing her way between people or, when necessary, loudly demanding they let her pass.

Waynton finished his drink, then said to Diana: 'At first I wondered why you kept interrupting her. Then I realized you were trying to head her off from asking me why I wasn't in prison.'

'She's a tongue that just can't stop clacking.'

'She can't clack much over what she's learned from me.'

'Are you really that naïve? By this time tomorrow she'll have convinced herself and most of the residents that you all but confessed to her.'

A middle-aged couple, the man dressed casually, the woman in a beautifully embroidered blouse and long silk skirt, moved round a group of people to come in sight of Diana and Waynton. The man smiled and began to approach, the woman murmured something and hung back, but then realized her husband had placed them in a situation from which there was no immediate escape.

'Hullo, Diana,' said the man. 'How's the world treating you?'

'As seldom as it can manage.'

The woman smiled briefly and nervously.

The man said to Waynton: 'Have you seen the Lamborghini that's going around the place? What a car!'

'Much too fragile when the going gets rough. I'll settle for the new Aston Martin when I've won the pools. Performance and lasting power.'

'The male ego, which has to rush around being noisy and brave!' said Diana. 'Put either of you in one of those cars and there'd be an accident within half an hour.'

The man laughed. 'Thank you for those few kind words.'

'I think I ought to have a word with Agnes,' said the woman, in her over-articulated voice. 'Come on, Will.'

The man said awkwardly: 'When the boss says move, we all move. Be seeing you around.' He followed his wife.

A maid refilled their glasses. As she left, Waynton said: 'Reading between the lines, which isn't exactly difficult, I'd say I've become bad news.'

'They're just . . .' Diana stopped, accepting the fact that it would be ridiculous to deny that the woman had been very uneasy at the meeting.

'You did try to warn me.'

'And you refused to listen. Harry, I'm bored. I never was very good at parties and when there are a whole lot of people I don't want to talk to, it's worse. Let's go back to my place and have a scratch meal?'

'Or to put it more simply, turn tail and run?'

'Can't you ever understand . . .?'

'That there is a time when one should turn? Run today and live to fight tomorrow. I'd rather . . .'

'It's all too obvious what you'd rather do. Crack your bloody thick head against the nearest brick wall. Come on, we're off.'

'Wouldn't it be better if I sidled out on my own?'

'Sometimes I could crack your head for you.' She took

his glass from him and put that down, with hers, on a table. She tucked her arm round his.

They walked, aware of the interest which followed them, to where Mrs McKay was talking to one of the maids. The maid left as they approached. 'I'm afraid we must be on our way,' said Diana.

'Must you?' she answered, her round, pleasant face giving little hint of the keen brain behind it. 'Stay on and have a quick bite first – the food's all ready inside.'

'Thanks, but we really must go.'

Waynton saw Diana into her car and helped her to back out of the field being used as a temporary car-park, then returned to his Mobylette.

The journey was a short one, but for him not quick because it was largely uphill: by the time he had walked the bike up the last stretch where the road was too steep for riding, Diana had parked her car in the garage and had gone indoors.

When she opened the front door for him she handed him a glass. 'Things never seem quite so serious after an extra glass of champagne.'

'I had two glassfuls at the McKays and . . .'

'Third time lucky.'

He stepped inside. 'D'you know what? Despite all you'd said, I was still certain that except for one or two of the stupider types, people tonight would go out of their way to be friendly to me to show what they thought of the crazy rumours.'

She said, as she led the way into the sitting-room: 'You've never lived in a tiny community before, have you? I tried to tell you that everything gets blown up out of all proportion and rumours become facts even before they've had time to be distorted.'

'I still think we ought to have stayed on.'

She sat on the settee. 'It always has to be direct confrontation with you men, doesn't it? I'm bigger and stronger than you are. Why is it cowardly to avoid an unpleasantness if it can be avoided without trouble? Look, you must be able to imagine what kind of stories are going the rounds about you and Betty. Horrible, hateful stories, thought up because people out here haven't anything to do and all day to do it in. If you insist on continually facing them, they'll go on gossiping. If you cool it and don't stick your neck out, they'll soon shut up because they can't concentrate on anything for long without a reason.'

He paced the floor. 'What really gets me is how they can be so bloody silly as to think I'd have an affair with Betty.'

'She was quite attractive.'

'That's the only essential criterion?'

'It's a reasonably common one.'

'And they think I'm the kind of bloke who'd tumble her when Bill was upstairs . . .' He stopped and swung round. 'Do you?'

'Do you have to ask?'

'No,' he said, his voice suddenly calm. 'Of course I don't.'

She knew fresh fear. If only he weren't quite so certain. If only someone else was known to have been friendly with Betty . . .

CHAPTER XVII

On the Sunday Alvarez had identified Cifret and by noon on Monday the lawyers had reluctantly declared themselves satisfied over the proposed application for extradition. Soon, he thought, he would be free to return to the sun, colour, and life.

From a sense of duty, he had invited Fletcher to lunch at the hotel. He wanted to like the man, yet no matter how hard he tried he found himself unable to do so. There was a coldness of spirit about the D.I. which seemed to freeze all points of emotional contact. For Alvarez, he was the epitome of all the heroes of the British wartime films which were often shown on television on Saturday nights. Captain, captain, the rear gunner's shot and is dying, the tailplane's gone, the hull's on fire amidships, and another night fighter's about to attack: it's terrible. Just calm down and make your report correctly, Smithers. There's no call to get excited.

'I've arranged this afternoon for us to go over HQ,' said Fletcher. There was a trace of patronage in his voice when he added: 'I thought it would give you the chance to see a really modern set-up.'

'That would be most interesting,' replied Alvarez politely.

'You won't have had the chance to see the latest computer techniques in police work.'

'As a matter of fact, in Palma we . . .'

'Now take the question of time correlation, statement time-check, and statement and information cross-check charts. You draw these up for every major crime and that takes a lot of time, doesn't it? But we just feed the information into the computer and dial the machine for the answers we want.'

Alvarez accepted it would save a lot of time, even when one knew what all these things were.

'We'll leave here at three so that you'll have plenty of time to look around the place.'

'Three o'clock this afternoon, señor?'

'That's right. Why?'

'But surely you will be having a little siesta?'

Fletcher looked at him in amazement.

They stood in the centre of a room over forty feet long and thirty wide, which with the exception of a small control room was filled from floor to ceiling with shelves which were packed with files. Fletcher spoke with the enthusiasm of the dedicated statistician. 'We've over twenty-three thousand five hundred of our own files here. They cover current crime, all cleared-up crime and all cases put on ice over the past ten years, all investigations undertaken over the past five years whether conclusive or not, and details of all major national crimes over the past two years. The contents of the files aren't on tapes, but a précis of the facts are and so cross-references are available at the press of a button.

'The benefits are obvious. Instead of men spending hours wading through the files and the index of cross-references, becoming bored and careless, now a few buttons are pressed, file numbers are given, and all relevant information is immediately available. How about a practical example? Tell me, what was the last case of sudden and unexplained death you've experienced on your island?'

Alvarez, who'd allowed his thoughts to wander and had

been thinking wistfully of the bed back in his bedroom at the hotel, hurriedly said: 'Just recently, señor, a woman died from what appeared to be some form of poisoning. The circumstances suggested there was a strong motive for murder. But then the post-mortem told us that she'd died from mytilotoxin which is a poison which comes from mussels.'

'That's not at all bad because there won't have been many poisonings by mussels and to pick up a reference to a previous case could take a long time. Now – shall we time ourselves?'

'By all means,' agreed Alvarez politely.

'Fifteen hundred and forty-five hours, thirty seconds. Go!' He walked quickly across to the control room and went inside. 'First, the index. P for poisoning and then the sub-heading of mussels.' With smooth, economical movements he picked out a large book from among six others, placed this on a small table, and opened it: it seemed fitting that he should have opened it only one page away from the one he sought. 'Three-six-four-one-five.' He crossed to a typewriter-like computer input machine, switched it on, and typed out the numbers. There was a brief pause and then the golf-ball head typed out a reference number. 'ATX stroke one-four-six stroke G stroke six-three-two-seven-one,' he read out.

He left the control room at a very brisk rate. 'ATX is down here,' he said over his shoulder, as he made his way between two rows of shelving on the left-hand side of the room. 'The heading signifies cases opened and then closed because there proved to be no cause for further investigation . . . One-four-six – first section. G, third shelf up. Six-three-two-seven-one, file number. And here it is.' He pulled out a file. 'Time now fifteen hundred and forty-seven hours, forty-one seconds. Time from initiation to execution, two minutes and eleven seconds.'

'Wonderful!' exclaimed Alvarez. He began to yawn and hurriedly tried to smother it.

'Let's see what we've pulled out.' Fletcher opened the file and quickly read through the summary on the title page. 'Fairly typical of the kind of case where the facts prove there's no case for a full investigation. A rich wife and a husband who was willed everything. Wife died from a violent illness. Doctor reported matters to the coroner who ordered a PM. Cause of death, mytilotoxin from eating contaminated mussels. Case closed.' He handed the folder to Alvarez.

Alvarez read the name Mrs Monica Heron.

CHAPTER XVIII

They were in Fletcher's office and now Detective Chief-Inspector Udell was seated behind his desk. Alvarez, on a chair between the desks, felt rather like a shuttlecock.

'Coincidences do happen,' said Udell, who was a serious, even ponderous man.

'Indeed, señor. But . . .'

'Coincidences happen every day of the week,' said Fletcher, with tired patience.

'Of course, but from the beginning I have had a feeling about this case that I have told you about. Something is very wrong with things as they appear.'

'A feeling for a case is not really all that reliable an indication, you know,' said Fletcher.

'How can I explain it? All the facts say one thing, yet all the time there is a small part of my brain which says something else.'

'And what does this . . . this small part of your brain say?'

Alvarez shrugged his shoulders. 'But I do not know,' he said, almost despairingly. 'Señor Heron's wife dies from eating mussels. Then he comes to Mallorca to live and with him is an attractive woman. He becomes seriously ill and dies after a long illness. His friend, Señorita Stevenage, dies from eating mussels. Does that not make you think?'

'It makes me think I'd rather not eat mussels,' said Fletcher.

'Señor, we must look at this carefully. You said Señora Heron was rich?'

'Her will was probated at two hundred and fifty-three thousand four hundred and sixteen pounds, fifty-three p.' Alvarez struggled with the task of mentally translating that sum into pesetas. 'That is about thirty-six million pesetas. It is a very great sum. And Señor Heron inherited everything?'

'There were one or two small bequests, but otherwise he inherited the entire estate. There were no children of the marriage.'

'And no death duties since the bequest was from wife to husband,' said Udell.

Alvarez spoke slowly, striving not to be, by inference, critical of their past actions. 'Señors, you must have thought to yourselves, here we have a rich woman who dies and a husband who inherits, so we must investigate very closely?'

'Of course. That is why there is a file on the case.'

'And you investigated and it seemed the death was natural. But now that I have told you about Señorita Stevenage, do you not perhaps wonder whether maybe you missed something?'

Fletcher spoke coldly: 'We missed nothing. Mrs Monica Heron died from mytilotoxin poisoning. The facts of the case are incontrovertible. Both the wife and the husband were taken ill, she more seriously than he. He managed to call their doctor who had them both rushed to hospital. She died and he survived. There was an autopsy and the cause of death was found to be mytilotoxin poisoning. There was thus no further cause for us to investigate further.'

'Did the police question Señor Heron?'

'Of course, since he recovered sufficiently to be questioned before the results of the autopsy were to hand. He could tell us no more than that he'd bought some mussels and cooked them for his wife and himself because mussels were one of her favourite dishes. Soon after eating they both began to feel unwell and started vomiting. He thought at first that after they'd been sick they'd recover, but instead they became worse and so he called the doctor.' Fletcher leaned back in his chair. 'As a matter of interest, the mussels came from Spain.'

Had the positions been reversed, thought Alvarez, no Spaniard would have been so ill-mannered as to point out where the mussels had come from. 'Do you know what kind of a person Señora Heron was?'

'There's no indication of that in the file, except as regards physical description. She was five feet seven tall and weighed seventeen stone.'

'Can you tell me what that weight would be in kilos?'

'I suppose it's here somewhere – we're supposed to be going metric.' It was clear that Fletcher was no lover of the metric system. He opened the folder and looked through the pages inside, soon finding the figure. 'Near enough one hundred and eight kilos.'

'Then she was a large woman! Were she and her husband happy together? Did he have any lady friends while she was still alive? Did he have a job, or did he live on her money?'

'I'm sorry, but as I've just said, the report doesn't list those facts since they proved to be irrelevant.'

'Señor, as a very great favour might I speak to someone who can tell me these things?'

'I really can't see there's any point . . .'

'Tom, you can surely lay that on for Mr Alvarez,' said Udell.

Fletcher's mouth tightened.

Alvarez, in the larger of the two hotel bars, was mourn-

fully thinking about how much a very small brandy had
just cost him when a man came up and said: 'Are you Mr
Alvarez from Mallorca? I'm Detective-Sergeant Inchcape,
from Menton Cross.'

Alvarez shook hands. 'Would you like a drink, señor?'

'A half-and-half would slide down a treat.' Realizing
that Alvarez had not understood the order, he gave it
direct to the barman. 'I've been told to come here and give
you all the gen on the Heron case. I gather you think
things may not be quite as straightforward as they seemed?'

Alvarez studied the detective-sergeant and judged him
to be a man with a strong sense of humour and the ability
to accept the possibility of having made a mistake. 'I will
tell you the exact truth. I just do not know. All there is is
this feeling . . .' He shrugged his shoulders.

'I know what you mean. Something stinks, but you
don't know what.'

Not quite the expression he would have used in this
case, thought Alvarez. The barman pushed a tumbler of
beer across and he paid for this, then suggested they went
over to one of the tables.

As soon as they were seated, Inchcape raised his glass.
'Here's to everyone.' He drank. 'That's better! . . . Now,
what can I do for you?'

'Please, you can tell me everything you know about the
case.'

'OK. And I'll give you the facts as I finally knew them,
not in the order in which I learned them. She was nearly
ten years older than he was and had inherited a fortune
from her father: he had worked in an insurance office
before they married, but never reached much of a position.
They met at a party and it's pretty obvious he decided
he'd nab her if he could. She was known as a rather dull
woman, without looks, who'd messed up her life by

staying at home to look after her father. Heron was a
bachelor with a reputation for chasing the skirt and very
sure of his own charm. Three months after the party they
became engaged, three months after that they were
married. People thought she was being a fool, but she was
more than old enough to know what she wanted to do.

'It's difficult to be certain now – people seldom accurately remember their past judgements – but it does seem
as if the marriage was happy for the first four to five years.
Then something happened. No one seems to know what,
but I'd give you ten to one that she discovered he was two-
timing her. There were rows, reconciliations, and more
rows. She became unusually firm and threatened to chuck
him out of the house, then lacked the courage actually to
do so – probably because she was still in love with him.
She suddenly began to eat like crazy. Her GP became
worried and persuaded her to see a psychiatrist and he
diagnosed something he called compensatory hunger: to
you or me that means she was desperately unhappy
because her husband was fooling around and so by way of
compensation she ate and ate. Seems a damn funny way of
going about life, but apparently it happens quite often.
So in next to no time she was a barrel and had lost any
looks she'd had – and because she'd become a barrel, he
lost whatever small interest he still had in her.

'He had been reasonably circumspect with his women
until now, but once she'd become fat he no longer seemed
to give a damn what she found out about him. He was seen
all over the place with one particular woman and the
tongues in the neighbourhood wagged themselves silly.
There was a tremendous row with his wife, she told him
she wasn't going to stand it any longer and he took fright
and swore to mend his ways. And in order to prove that
despite everything he did still love her, he became all

affectionate and cooked her all the meals she specially liked – I suppose he reckoned the way to her money-bags was now through her stomach. And that's how he came to cook the mussels in a sauce of garlic and tomato. Sounds horrible to me, but then I'm a fish and chips man. They hadn't eaten long when she said she wasn't feeling at all well and as he was also beginning to be a bit queer he decided they ought to take something to settle their stomachs. He gave her some stomach pills they'd got – innocuous, they were checked – but they didn't do any good and she got worse and suddenly he became pretty ill as well. He managed to phone their GP and then collapsed. They were both rushed to hospital where she died and he survived.

'In her will she'd left everything to him, barring a few small legacies. A month after the funeral he put the house up for sale and managed to catch the market on the up-swing so he sold it for a pretty high price. He left the neighbourhood and none of his friends or acquaintances saw him after that. In fact, it's a safe bet they didn't even know he'd gone to Mallorca until they saw the notice in the papers – always assuming there was one.'

Alvarez spoke urgently. 'Señor, nothing could more suggest murder than a rich wife who is no longer attractive and a husband who is running after other women.'

'Check! It had me all inquisitive, I can tell you. But in this country any death which seems at all suspicious or where the doctor hasn't been in attendance very recently is referred to the coroner who can order a post-mortem. There was a post-mortem on Mrs Heron and that found that she died from mussel poisoning.'

'Do you know what was the name of the woman the señor was seeing just before the señora died?'

'Elizabeth Stevenage.'

'But ... but Betty Stevenage came out to Mallorca with Señor Heron and after he died from heart trouble she decided to leave the island and then she died – from mussel poisoning.'

Inchcape said: 'Now there's a coincidence!' Then he drank and emptied his glass.

'It cannot be a coincidence: I swear to that. Both women must have been murdered.'

'Didn't you have a PM on Betty Stevenage?'

'There was one, yes, but the body was not found for a month and by then there had been so much putrefaction that no precise cause of death could be ascertained. All the surrounding circumstances suggested mussel poisoning. Now that I know this, though, I also know ...' He paused, then corrected himself. 'I can be almost certain that she was murdered.'

'Are you sure you can go that far? After all, as I've told you, Mrs Heron wasn't murdered, she died from mytilotoxin poisoning. Accidental death.'

'The post-mortem result has to be wrong. I must speak to the pathologist and try to show him that he has missed something. Any man can miss something, even a man like Detective-Inspector Fletcher.'

'I think you're wrong there.' Inchcape smiled. He stood. 'Let's have the other half, then. What was yours?'

CHAPTER XIX

In Menton Cross, a smaller town than Bearstone but with far more character, the mortuary was a modern two-storey building not far from divisional HQ. The post-mortem room, beautifully equipped and looking like an operating theatre with its central adjustable table under an enclosed pod of overhead lights, was to the right of the building and behind this was a small office. Professor Keen spoke to Alvarez in here.

He was a friendly man, with a round, smiling face, and an air of quiet competence. He shook hands with Alvarez and Detective-Sergeant Inchcape, then indicated the two chairs which had been set out in front of the desk. He settled on the edge of the desk, took off his spectacles, and rubbed the side of his nose where the rests had irritated the skin.

Inchcape said: 'Mr Alvarez wanted to have a word with you about the Heron case, sir. There are one or two facts he needs to check up on because they may be connected with a case he's handling in Mallorca.'

'Yes, you mentioned that over the phone.' He reached across the desk, opened a folder, and brought out a sheet of paper which he read very briefly. 'OK. Fire away.'

'Señor, in Mallorca a woman has died from mytilotoxin poisoning after eating mussels and her name was Betty Stevenage. She came to the island with Señor Heron, who died a month before because of his heart.'

'I see.' He replaced his spectacles.

'It would seem a very great coincidence.'

'I'd agree.'

'So I am wondering . . . Can it really be a coincidence?'

Keen slid off the desk and went round to sit. He pulled
the folder round, studied one of the papers left inside it,
then looked up at Alvarez. 'Presumably what you'd really
like to know is if there's any chance I made a mistake in
my autopsy on Monica Heron?'

'I regret the necessity, señor.'

'Don't give it a thought – no one else ever does. I can
answer you very briefly. It is quite certain that Monica
Heron died from mytilotoxin poisoning, as a result of
eating contaminated mussels.'

'There remains no possibility of doubt?'

'I think the best way of answering you is to give you a
brief résumé of all the facts. As always, when this case was
referred to me I asked for the full background. The two
people had eaten mussels in a prepared sauce. The first
symptoms of illness began not long afterwards. Both
suffered prickling in the fingers and tingling in the throat
and mouth and this tingling spread over their bodies,
causing considerable distress. Heron described the
sensation as feeling as if his hands were made of fur: this is
a well documented symptom, sometimes described as the
"glove feeling". They suffered cold sweats and shivering,
which led up to a deadly chill – as if all the blood in their
bodies had turned to ice water. They suffered agonizing
pains around the body and head, in particular about the
heart. Mrs Heron suffered circulatory paralysis and
cardiac distress after about three hours.

'Now these symptoms are wholly consistent with
poisoning from two entirely different sources. The first is
mytilotoxin. It's a poison which is found in some mussels
and is particularly connected with their breeding season,
that is during the summer months. Some places grow
mussels far more likely to contain this poison than others

and to the best of my knowledge no one has ever yet been able to explain on scientific grounds why. The most famous example is South Darkpoint on the east coast – here, the taking of mussels is now banned from April through to September. As one might expect, there are people fool enough to ignore the ban and most of them suffer no ill effects, but some suffer mild symptoms of poisoning, a few become very ill, and there is the occasional death. Naturally, if the mussel is dead before being prepared, then the danger is far worse.

'The second form of poison is the alkaloid aconite which comes from the monkshood plant. The roots of this are occasionally eaten in mistake for horse radish, usually with fatal results. As a matter of interest, although it is a deadly poison, in therapeutic doses it is very effective in relieving some pains, such as neuralgias. A lot of poisons have this dual identity – rather a fascinating subject.

'I've mentioned all this at some length to show why, when I commenced the PM, I could be reasonably certain that Mrs Heron had died from either mytilotoxin or aconitine poisoning. Examination showed she had died from mytilotoxin and there was no trace whatsoever of aconite in her body.

'I asked Mr Heron, who made an excellent recovery, where he'd bought the mussels and he told me from a shop in Soho. They'd been in their shells and imported from Spain. His wife had developed a very considerable appetite and he bought quite a quantity and cooked and served these at the one meal. His estimate was that she'd eaten at least four-fifths of the mussels, so it's no wonder she was taken fatally ill since it's quite possible that the majority of these mussels were poisonous.

'The authorities were informed and they investigated the matter. As I understand it, the Spanish exporters claim that their mussels could not possibly be poisonous and refuse to accept any blame. However, Mrs Heron was killed by mytilotoxin poisoning so one has to accept the fact that a mistake must have been made.'

Alvarez, his shoulders hunched, stared down at his shoes. 'It is very strange,' he said, after a while. 'When a man marries a woman for her money and seeks his pleasures elsewhere and she threatens to throw him out of the house if he does not behave himself, then dies a violent death, it is very strange to discover she died accidentally.'

The pathologist smiled briefly. 'You sound as if you're a cynic.'

A cynic? He hoped he was not that. A cynic was contemptuous of people: he believed in people. But as a detective . . .

Detective-Inspector Fletcher, not a hair out of line, tie exactly centred, shirt uncreased, suit immaculate, met Alvarez just outside the main entrance to county HQ. 'I hear you had a wasted morning,' he said, not without a hint of malice.

Alvarez, certain he looked as dowdy as Fletcher looked smart, said: 'It was very kind of you to arrange everything.'

'I gather the PM was properly conducted after all?'

'Indeed, señor.'

'It's one of the advantages of this country. We can always accept the PM report without the slightest hesitation.'

'It was just that it seemed to me I must find out for certain about Señora Heron.'

Fletcher nodded. Clearly, one had to make allowances for foreigners who, of necessity, lacked experience.

*

The plane turned slowly and the starboard wing dipped to let Alvarez look down at the dramatic northern coastline. They swept over mountains and crossed the plain and as they slowly descended, their shadow playing tag with the Don Quixote windmills, he could see patchwork fields, a few animals, houses sleeping in the sunshine, and empty roads. The island of calm. So different from that grey, over-populated, frenetic island he had left only two hours before.

He heard the grinding noise of the wheels being lowered and he closed his eyes. Most crashes occurred on take-off or landing. Sometimes a few passengers survived and that was why he had chosen a seat by one of the emergency exits.

There was a slight bump, a change of engine note, and they were down and safe. He opened his eyes and looked out at the airport buildings, fronted by flowers. Home. Sunshine.

There was no one there to meet him, but he was neither surprised nor bothered, even though a Telex message had been sent through. Probably the Guardia detailed to come in and fetch him had forgotten . . . These things happened.

He went out of the main building and could feel the sunshine soaking through him, driving out the dismal damp which had accumulated over the past four days. He crossed to the waiting tourist buses and found one which was going to Puerto Llueso. The driver was asleep, sprawled out in one of the double seats and Alvarez sat on the other side of the gangway. He closed his eyes and gratefully let the world drift by.

When he walked into the house and Dolores saw him, she shouted: 'You're back!' She rushed forward and hugged him. Then she stepped back. 'But so pale and

thin! They've been starving you. Thank God I've prepared a solid dinner. There's beans and ham and after
that chicken and rice with peppers and garlic . . .'

'Say no more. By the time I go to bed I'll have put on
all the weight I've lost.'

Juan and Isabel entered the house and after their
initial excitement waited with an expectation which was
not disappointed. He gave Isabel a pair of gold ear-rings
in the shape of horseshoes and Juan a working model kit
of a tank. Jaime arrived half an hour later and after
shaking hands and speaking a few warm words of greeting
he hurried through to the dining-room and brought back
two glasses filled with brandy.

'You're not going to drink all that before the meal,' said
Dolores belligerently.

'When a man returns home,' replied Jaime, 'he needs a
drink to clear his throat.'

'But not one big enough to drown it.' She was, however,
smiling.

When Alvarez went up to his bedroom he opened the
shutters which had been closed throughout the day to keep
out the sun and he looked over the rooftops at Puig
Antonia. The hermitage on the crown of the sugar loaf
mountain, which housed the remains of Santa Antonia,
was still just visible since dusk had not yet quite become
night. Santa Antonia, he said silently, if I were not so old
and short of breath I would climb up tomorrow to light a
candle for you in thanks for bringing me safely back here
to the people I love and who love me.

Alvarez dialled the Institute of Forensic Anatomy and
then propped his feet up on the desk. A gecko looking
round the outside corner of the window saw him and in
one quick squiggle of movement disappeared.

When the connection was made, he asked to speak to Professor Fortunato.

'What is it?' asked a sharp, crackling voice which suggested a man of very small temper.

'Señor, this is Inspector Alvarez from Llueso. I'm sorry to bother you, but because of something I've recently learned I'd very much like to ask you a question concerning the autopsy on Señorita Stevenage.'

'Well – what's the question?'

'Señor, could the deceased have died from aconitine poisoning, not mytilotoxin poisoning? The reason for asking is that there's now evidence to suggest this was possible.'

'Wait, please, while I look at my file.'

He lit a cigarette. It would be ironic if he discovered that it was the Mallorquin post-mortem which had made the mistake.

'Have you read the report?'

'Of course, señor.'

'I've nothing more to add to what I wrote then.'

'Señor, I've just returned from England and over there I discovered that Señor Heron, the man with whom the señorita was living before he died from natural causes, had been married to a wealthy woman and she died last year from mytilotoxin poisoning. It seems to be too great a coincidence truly to be one. And while I was in England I learned that the symptoms of the two poisonings are similar.'

'Did you there also learn that tests for aconitine poisoning are confined to biological assay dependant on the isolation of the aconite, which is destroyed by putrefaction?'

'No, señor.'

'Then before you again decide to question an expert's

findings, I suggest you make certain you have mastered your own brief.'

He replaced the receiver. Fool, he thought, meaning himself. According to the records, Señorita Stevenage had died a natural death. So why had he needlessly stirred up trouble? He let his head sink down on to his chest. What strange bubble of perversity could possess him? A belief in justice? But true justice was incapable of definition because it could only exist subjectively. A love of the truth? At times truth could hurt so much more than lies. So why . . .?

CHAPTER XX

Alvarez stepped into Francisca's house and called out. She hurried into the entrance room. 'I didn't know you were back. Come on into the other room and pour yourself a drink and then tell me all about England. Is it like it is on the telly? Did you see the palace and the guards . . .?'

He had one drink and then another and it was time for luncheon and by chance she had prepared a dish for Miguel which she knew was a favourite of his . . . He ate very well and after the meal she insisted he sat in the most comfortable chair in the sitting-room to digest.

It was after five when he awoke, to find Francisca sitting opposite him and embroidering a sheet. He hurried to his feet. 'I must get moving fast.'

'Why?' she asked peacefully. 'What will have turned up which can't wait while you pause to clear your mind and drink a cup of coffee with a slice of sponge with angel's hair jam to go with the coffee?'

'Angel's hair jam?'

'That's right.' She looked artlessly at him. 'Didn't Dolores once tell me you'd something of a sweet tooth?'

Most things, he thought, as he sat down again and settled in the chair, sorted themselves out if only one left them alone to do so.

It was while he was eating his third slice of sponge cake that he said: 'Francisca, you remember Señorita Stevenage?'

'What a peculiar question. But of course I remember her.'

'Didn't you once tell me that she'd had a dog?'

'That's right. It was really jolly, but had such long trailing hair it was always getting that awful grass stuck in it and what a job it was then to untangle its coat.'

'Was she fond of it?'

'It was absolutely ridiculous. When all's said and done, a dog is only a dog, not a child. Yet she'd talk to it as if it were her only son and cuddle it in her arms . . . We can't all be the same, which I suppose is just as well, but if I'd been her I'd have given more of my affection to the man I was living with and less to my dog.'

'Have I got it right that the dog died very suddenly?'

'I arrived at the finca one morning and there was the señorita, in floods of tears. I can remember thinking, so it's happened at last. Well, the señor had finally found peace. Then I heard him calling from upstairs. It gave me quite a turn, I can tell you: just like hearing a voice coming up from a grave. So when she came downstairs and the tears were still falling I said, "What is the matter, señorita? Has you dear father died?" And she told me it was the dog. All those tears were for that little dog!'

'Did she know why it had died?'

'She'd no idea. One moment it had seemed all right, the next it had been violently sick and unable to stand.'

'Have you any idea what happened to the body?'

'She told the gardener to bury it. I seem to remember there was even some form of tombstone.'

'Who was their gardener?'

'It was only old Rafael Yarza who came one morning a week. D'you know what he charged them? A hundred and ten pesetas an hour! And that was for leaning on his mattock and staring at the land. But they never seemed to worry that their money was just standing around, doing nothing.'

'Where does he live?'

'Somewhere along the Calle Mostet.'

'Well, I really must be getting along now.' He stood up. 'Thanks for everything. I've eaten and drunk far too much.'

'And had a bit of a sleep, which you needed more than anything else.'

He left and drove past shuttered houses to Calle Mostet, a narrow street without pavements which sloped quite steeply upwards. Some children were playing hop-scotch and from one of the girls he learned which was Yarza's house.

Yarza lived with his daughter and her family and from the way in which she spoke it was clear that at times his presence became resented. 'Dad's out at the back so if you want to talk to him you'd better go through. And tell him he left his stuff all over the front room again.'

He went through the kitchen and out to the courtyard. This was small, but the beds were filled with colour and in the centre were two orange trees, leaves dark green and the following winter's crop thick on the branches.

For a Mallorquin, Yarza was a large man: he'd just begun to bow and shrink from age. He hadn't shaved that day, but his clothes were clean, if darned, and his shoes were well polished. He studied Alvarez, but didn't speak.

Alvarez examined the nearer orange tree. 'What d'you do to the soil to get the trees to grow like this?'

'Plant 'em over a dead cat and then give 'em lots of dung, that's what. None of them artificials.' Yarza hawked and spat, showing his contempt for artificial fertilizers.

'I'm from the Cuerpo General . . .'

'Bloody hell, d'you think I don't know who you are?'

'Then maybe you also know why I'm here?'

He shrugged his shoulders.

'I'm interested in the dog which belonged to Señorita Stevenage.'

'That? More like a ball of muddied wool than a dog; that thing never earned its grub.'

'Francisca tells me it died very suddenly. I wondered if you knew why it died?'

'It was ill, it died. Who ever knows any more than that?'

'But it died so quickly and unexpectedly.'

'Some animals die slow, some die quick. There ain't nothing you can do about it.'

'D'you think it could have been poisoned?'

He rubbed the lobe of his right ear with a thumb and forefinger which were horny with thick skin. 'How would I know? If an animal's dying d'you think I get down beside it and ask why?'

'Where did you bury it?'

He hesitated, then said: 'Out behind the house.'

'Whereabouts outside?'

'Back beyond the pig shed. I don't remember exactly.'

'You don't remember?' Alvarez said disbelievingly.

Yarza appeared to become wholly interested in one of the orange trees.

'Let's go to Ca'n Ibore and find out if you can do better than that. And bring a mattock.'

'I can't move on account of me bones are killing me. The doc says I'm to rest.'

'You can rest all you like as soon as we've found the grave.'

Yarza stared at Alvarez with dislike, then began to shuffle his way into the house.

They left the village by the eastern bridge, passing over the rocky, dry bed of the torrente, now partially over-grown with weeds although in January it had surged with deep flood water.

On the land behind Ca'n Ibore, where no one had
ever cleared it, maquis scrub grew among boulders and
outcrops of rock. As they came in sight of it, a goat, neck
bell clanging unmusically, hurried away, movements
ungainly because its legs were hobbled.

'Where should we start looking?' asked Alvarez.

'I told you, I've forgotten.'

'And I'm telling you that I'm not as simple as I look. If
you'd planted half a dozen melon seeds in the middle of a
wood you'd remember precisely where they were six
months later. So come on, where did you bury the dog?'

'I don't remember.'

He was a peasant himself, but that didn't stop him
sometimes cursing a peasant's stubbornness. He walked
slowly along a narrow, winding path which had at some
time been blasted through the scrub and rock. Yarza
would have considered the job of burying the dog a
ridiculous one and therefore he would have taken as little
trouble over it as possible. He would have looked for an
accessible pocket of earth, just deep enough . . . As he
rounded an evergreen oak, Alvarez saw a small boulder
in front of which was some earth in which was a small
cross. On the cross, carefully carved, was the inscription:
'Sandy'. He turned. 'Was the dog called Sandy?'

'What if it was?'

'Then we've found the grave. So now you can dig up the
body.'

Yarza used the mattock to scoop through the earth and
it was soon clear that no dog had ever been buried there.

Alvarez took a pack of cigarettes from his pocket and
offered it. When they were both smoking, he said: 'All
right, I now know why you didn't want to tell me where
the dog was supposed to be buried. So having got this far,
you'd better tell me what you did do with the body.'

Yarza leaned on the handle of the mattock and smoked. After a while he cleared his throat and said: 'She wanted me to bury him out here because that's where he used to like to chase around. I tried to tell her, there ain't enough earth to bury anything: it's all rock. Wouldn't listen. I wasn't going to kill myself breaking up them rocks, so I told her I put it here. Knew she'd never check. She had the cross made in the village and I wedged it up in the earth. It made her happy.'

'And what did you do with the body?'

'Chucked it down a hole.'

'Let's see the hole.'

The mountains and foothills were limestone, honeycombed by an unrecorded number of caves and holes: ten metres out from the shed through which they had earlier come was a fissure in the ground, shaped like a shield, three-quarters of a metre across at its greatest width.

'They used to chuck their tins down there,' said Yarza, for once volunteering information.

'Look,' said the younger Guard, as he stared resentfully down at the fissure in the ground, 'I didn't join the force to go and kill myself pot-holing.'

'Don't worry,' replied Alvarez, tying a rope round the other's waist, 'I promise to see your mother gets your medal.'

'Why don't you bloody go down yourself if you want this stinking dog so badly?'

'I'm too fat.'

'Drink less booze.'

'Come on, lad, you volunteered for the job.'

The second Guard laughed, making the first one swear. They lowered him down into the hole and he landed on a load of empty tins, amidst a clatter.

Alvarez hunkered down on his heels. 'Can you see the dog?'

'D'you mind waiting until I can find somewhere safe to stand? It's like a bloody roller-coaster down here.' As if to prove his words correct, he slipped amidst a further clatter of tins. Eventually he found a secure foothold and he switched on the torch and shone the beam around the small cave. 'There it is.'

'Is there much of the body left?'

'It looks like it's all left. Hey, what kind of a dog was it – a mop dog?'

'Stand clear. I'm dropping the shovel and basket down. And go carefully – I want that dog up here as undamaged as possible.'

They hauled the rubber basket up. When Alvarez untied the rope and the sides of the basket sprang open he saw that the dog was not a mess of putrefaction, as he'd expected, but was in shape and form clearly a Yorkshire terrier.

The forensic scientist rang Alvarez late Friday afternoon. 'What happened is what we call mummification. Dry heat when there's an accompanying current of air can prevent bacterial decomposition and therefore putrefaction. The dog must have been slap in a current of air which reached the bottom of the cave. There was only a little mould and no damage from insects.

'Most of the interior organs were in reasonable condition and I was able to isolate and identify a small amount of aconite.'

Alvarez whistled.

'It's impossible to say accurately what amount of

poison was administered, but I'd guesstimate this at about one twentieth of a grain – roughly the fatal dose for an adult.'

'Have you told Professor Fortunato all this?'

'Yes, I have. And his comment is that it doesn't change anything in respect of Señorita Stevenage. Her body was in far too advanced a stage of decomposition for there to be the slightest chance of tracing aconite in it, even though it now seems likely that that is what killed her.'

Alvarez thanked the other and rang off.

Someone – a man – had been dining with her. He had had to get rid of all traces of his presence to avoid coming under suspicion and so he had washed up all he'd used during the meal, but before washing up he'd automatically swept the mussel shells and lemon into the waste bucket, forgetting in the stress of the moment the need to take these away with him to conceal the fact that he'd been present.

Medically, it could now never be proved that Señorita Stevenage had been poisoned and had not died from mytilotoxin, so the fact that the dog had been poisoned by aconite was irrelevant. Was this, then, the perfect murder?

CHAPTER XXI

Alvarez parked his car outside a shop which sold electrical goods and agricultural machinery. He crossed the road and went into the doctor's house and called out. Señora Roldán came out of a room on his right. She was dressed with as much, perhaps more, chic than when he had last seen her, in a frock which was patterned with colours which drifted one into the other like a Turner sunset. Her hair was beautifully fashioned, her make-up light but effective. More than ever he was struck by the two certainties which clearly lay behind her beauty: that she gave passionately of love, but that she had to love to offer passion.

'Señora, is the doctor in? If so, I'd be grateful for a quick word with him.'

'I'll find out. Do sit down while you're waiting.' Her foreign accent gave her words an attractive lilt.

Roldán, as smartly if more conventionally dressed than she had been, came into the hall from a room to the left. 'My wife tells me you want to see me?' He pulled back the sleeve of his lightweight coat to look at his watch.

'I'll not keep you long, señor.'

'All right,' he said abruptly, making it still clearer that he was one man on the island to whom time did mean something.

They went into the surgery and Roldán sat behind his large desk.

'Señor, during all the time you were attending Señor Heron you must have spoken to Señorita Stevenage?'

'Of course. I thought I made this clear last time . . .'

'Please bear with me. Did she talk to you about matters which had nothing to do with the señor? I'm thinking that when people are very upset they often talk about their affairs to try and calm themselves. Perhaps she spoke to you about the time when she lived in England?'

'There wasn't much social chit-chat because I tried to cut my visits as short as was reasonable. No, I can't say that I remember her ever mentioning England.'

'She never said that Señora Heron had most unfortunately died from mytilotoxin poisoning?'

'What's that?' he asked sharply.

'Señora Heron died very suddenly and there was a post-mortem which found the cause had been mytilotoxin poisoning. The señorita never told you this?'

Roldán shook his head. He looked bewildered. 'That . . . that's quite a coincidence.'

'I don't think it was a coincidence. You see, tests have just shown that Señorita Stevenage's dog, which died not long before the señorita herself, was poisoned with aconite.'

'Mother of God!'

'I have spoken to the people in Palma and they say that it doesn't matter what the dog died from, they can't go on from there to say that the señorita was also poisoned by aconite. The state in which her body was precludes any other finding than the original one. But I've no doubts. She had a second lover even while her first one was upstairs in the house, dying, and she had become jealous of this second lover. And because she was so jealous, he had to get rid of her, perhaps because he is married and could not risk trouble, perhaps because he had become fed up with her. So now you'll understand why I need to know if she ever spoke to you.'

Roldán shook his head.

'She never mentioned a single name?'

'I keep telling you, no. I was far too busy to spend my time gossiping.' Roldán began to tap on the desk with his fingers. 'If it's impossible ever to prove she was poisoned with aconite instead of dying from mytilotoxin, there can never be any certainty.'

'Doctor, there can be certainty without proof even if there can't be proof without certainty.'

As Alvarez drove along the rough track through the maquis scrub a crossbill flicked round the edge of a pine tree, banked, and disappeared behind another pine: a second later he heard the call of a nightjar. He parked and climbed out into the hot sunshine. From away on the right came the clatter of a number of bells – a flock of sheep or herd of goats – and from all directions came the shrilling of cicadas. Peace on the island of calm. Yet a woman had died violently at the hands of a man and the image of peace was a mirage.

Dunton, followed by his wife, came out of the bungalow on to the raised patio. 'Herlock Sholmes in person,' he boomed. He was wearing yachting-style clothes, but it was difficult to imagine him braving anything but a dead flat calm.

'I'm sorry to trouble you again, señor.'

'It's no trouble at all,' said his wife, and it was obvious that her husband's manner worried her. She had taken a great deal of trouble over her appearance, but she still looked as if she would have been more at home behind a bar.

Alvarez climbed up on to the raised patio.

'It's happy time by my sun,' said Dunton. 'And as I've never met a Mallorquin who doesn't drink like three fishes, what'll it be?'

'A coñac, please.'

'Jo, pour his nibs a large brandy and you can give me the same. Don't forget the ice this time, will you?'

Alvarez was not in favour of women's lib, but he would have welcomed her telling her husband that he could get his own drinks.

'Well, what's to do now? Been seeing suspicious things through your magnifying glass?' Dunton laughed.

'I have to ask you, señor, where you used to live in England?'

'Where I what? . . . As I've always said, out here the only things which seem to matter are the ones which don't matter a brass farthing. Apply for a residencia and they want to know the names of your great-grandparents. We were in Kent: Garden of England, they call it, but if you ask me it's got very bloody weedy.'

'Did you live near Menton Cross?'

'That place? That's so dead they pay out the old age pension at fifty-five. We were on the coast.'

Mrs Dunton returned to the room with three tall, frosted glasses on a silver clover-leaf tray. She handed the glasses around.

'You probably knew Señora Heron, who lived near to Menton Cross?'

'Never clapped eyes on the lady: always assuming she was one. Look, old man, you musn't judge the outside world by this little smudge of an island. Everything's so tiny here that three cars make a traffic jam. There are fifty million people in the British Isles.'

'But in Kent, señor, surely not so many?'

'One and a half million, less us two. I tell you, you're lucky if you know your next-door neighbours. Or bloody unlucky.' He laughed loudly.

Alvarez could easily understand how those grey houses

under grey skies so gripped a man's soul that he did not even try to speak to his neighbours. He said, while looking at Josephine Dunton: 'Señor, last time I was here I asked you if you were friendly with Señorita Stevenage and you said you weren't. But I have been told that in fact you were.'

'Who told you that load of bloody nonsense?' demanded Dunton with sudden anger.

Mrs Dunton spoke very earnestly. 'We really hardly knew her at all. She was so . . . well, so difficult to get on with.'

'Not one of your oo-le-là girls,' said Dunton, and he laughed, his good humour restored.

'Then this information is wrong?'

'Like everything else you hear on this island, hopelessly wrong. You ought to be used to that by now, old man.'

'Then perhaps you will tell me if you are friendly with Señora Carrington?'

'Her. She's too noblesse obliged for me and you can quote me any time you want. What I say is, one person's just as good as another and it's plain bloody ridiculous to put on airs.'

'It is very pleasant to hear an Englishman express such a view, señor.'

Dunton stared suspiciously at Alvarez, but the latter's bland expression reassured him. 'I speak as I think and always have done.'

Señora Dunton had shown no distress at the mention of Señora Carrington's name, Alvarez noted.

When Alvarez explained he wanted to question Elliott further, Avis Elliott made it quite plain that this time she was staying. She sat down in an armchair and said, in her commanding voice: 'Gordon can't help you, so there's absolutely no point in your bothering him again.'

Alvarez asked Elliott where they had lived in England.

'We had a house near Oxford,' she said.

'Did you ever travel to Kent, señor?'

'We had a cousin in Kent whom we visited quite often,' she answered.

'Did you know Señora Heron?'

'He did not.'

'Señor, you will remember you told me that you hardly knew Señorita Stevenage?'

'Of course he didn't,' she snapped.

'But I have been told that, in fact, you did know her quite well.'

'Stuff and nonsense!' Her voice rose.

'But if you did not know her, why should the señorita have been so interested in who you were going out with, Señor?'

'She wasn't.'

Alvarez sighed as he half turned. 'Señora, I can assure you . . .'

'My good man, that woman can't possibly have been interested. Gordon has never been out with her. He has never been out with anyone but me.'

'Not even with Señora Carrington?'

'Certainly not.'

No wonder, thought Alvarez, that England hadn't suffered a successful invasion in over nine hundred years.

Waynton turned away from the window in the sitting-room of his flat. 'The rumour was going around that the post-mortem proved she'd died naturally.' His tone became bitterly ironic. 'I was expecting to be socially rehabilitated.'

Alvarez, seated in one of the armchairs which looked as

if a generation of holidaymakers had misused it, said:
'The findings of the post-mortem, señor, were that there
was no proof that the señorita had been deliberately
poisoned.'

'The difference seems rather subtle.'

'But very important as now, when there is fresh evidence
so that I have to ask more questions.'

'Are you back to thinking she was murdered?'

'I am afraid it becomes more and more likely.'

Waynton sat down.

'Señor, if she were murdered then the murderer was
surely very friendly with her. So I ask again, who was she
friendly with and again there is never any name but
yours.'

'I've explained God knows how many times that I was
friendly with her because I was sorry for her. For her part,
she seemed always to make a point of talking to me. But I
wasn't having an affair with her and I didn't kill her.'

'Then she must have had another friend. What is his
name?'

'D'you think I wouldn't have told you long ago if I'd
known it? Look, I'll spell it out once more. No one really
liked her, largely because of her own attitude: she didn't
give, she was always reserved and often antagonistic. But
if she saw me around the town she'd come over and talk
and have a coffee or drink. Yet even with me she was still
reserved. She never said a single thing ever to suggest she
was friendly with any man other than Bill.'

'This is a small island, señor, as I have been very much
reminded today, and the English community is even
smaller. I am certain there are people here with sharp
tongues who know everything about everybody else's
business and have great pleasure in talking about it. Surely
if the señorita were so friendly as to be having an affair

with another man this would be known to someone who would talk about it? . . . But always it is only your name which is mentioned.'

Waynton spoke angrily. 'Maybe she was just too smart for the gossips.'

'I have thought of that. But I have also thought that a woman is never cynical about her love, as a man may be, because always her heart as well as her body is involved and therefore she cannot be cynically secretive. Had Señorita Stevenage loved another man she would have had to meet him, to smile and reassure him and be reassured by him, to touch and be touched by him.'

'When we met we talked about nothing more intimate or exciting than the weather or the rate of exchange. Smile? She hardly ever smiled: she seemed too bitter and unhappy. Touching? We kept our hands to ourselves.'

Alvarez slumped deeper into the chair and sighed. 'Señor, think very hard because if it was not you, there just has to have been another man.'

'I can think from now until Christmas and I won't come up with a name. Start looking at things the other way round. Why in the hell should I kill her? What possible motive could I have?'

'She was very upset because she was in love with a man whom she believed was too friendly with another woman. You, señor, are friendly with Señora Carrington, aren't you?'

'Don't start dragging her name into this filthy muddle.'

'Sometimes I cannot avoid doing what I do not wish to do . . . Do you believe that in truth Señor Dunton or Señor Elliott also is friendly with Señora Carrington?'

'I've told you before, she can't stand the sight of either of them.'

'Yet Señorita Stevenage asked you if she were out with

one of them. Why should she ask this if it were impossible?'

'I don't know now and I didn't know the last time you asked me.'

'It is a great pity that you cannot help me, señor.'

Waynton stared at the detective, whose face sometimes portrayed the dogged, bloody-minded stubbornness of a peasant. How did you convince such a man that his ideas were hopelessly wrong? How did you persuade him that in human nature there was no absolute? Obviously Betty had been able to have a lover and yet be separated from him, to look at him without their secret ceasing to be a secret, to defy and defeat the gossips . . .

How long ago was it since he and Diana had sat in this room, gay because the heavy shadows of suspicion which had covered him had been rolled back? Months? Or was it really less than a week?

CHAPTER XXII

The bungalow, raised a metre above the ground, was built in the shape of the letter U. Between the two arms was a swimming pool. Vives, his bronzed body tautly muscled, climbed the ladder at the deep end of the pool. When he crossed the tiled surround the water dripped off and dampened the tiles, but the heat was such that they were soon once more dry.

He towelled himself. 'Enrique, you should have a swim. It would tone up your body, which is getting as fat as a matanzas pig.'

'It's much more likely to kill me,' replied Alvarez, who stood within the shade of a brightly coloured beach umbrella.

A small girl crossed the patio to her father. She looked shyly at Alvarez, then tugged at her father's leg and said something in a low voice. Vives bent down, listened, straightened up and said: 'Matilde says, would you like some coffee?'

'I certainly would.'

The small girl hurried away and returned indoors. The two men sat on patio chairs and Alvarez stared across the pool at the orange and lemon trees and the vines, thick with grapes, which were beyond it. Vives came from peasant stock and had never forgotten that fact. He had made a great deal of money, but had not lost his sense of values. The land around the house was fertile and so he had not wasted it by filling it with flowers, as a foreigner would, but had planted fruit and vegetables.

They were silent for a time, content to be completely at

peace. Then finally Alvarez said: 'The dog belonging to Señorita Stevenage was killed by poison.'

'So I have heard.'

'The poison was aconite and the symptoms of this are very, very similar to those of mytilotoxin. When a body begins to decay the aconite is lost and then no one can be certain it was ever there. But I am certain. So again and again I have asked myself, why was she killed? I think of love because she had a lover, but she was a lonely woman and the only man who she is known to have been friendly with doesn't seem to be the kind of man to murder her by poisoning . . . Though can anyone really be certain of that? Then I wonder, why else do people murder? One answer is money. Señor Heron's wife, who died in England, was a very rich woman. Was much of his money out here?'

'Practically none at all. If there's thirty thousand pesetas in his estate by the end of the day I'll be surprised.'

'Where is his money, then?'

'Back in England, out in Switzerland, tucked away in the States. Where does a rich man put his money these days with inflation and devaluation?'

'There must be a will to suggest where it is?'

'I'm concerned only with Spain, you know that. And he didn't bother to make a Spanish will because he had almost no capital here. The furnished house was rented, the car was rented. The bank account was in both their names and when he died the señorita did as I had suggested and withdrew everything but the last few hundred pesetas which she put into an account in her own name.'

'And did she leave a will?'

'She made none through me.'

'So you can't really tell me anything about his money?'

'That's right.'

'Then I'll have to check with his bank to see if they've any ideas. D'you know which one he used?'

'Not off-hand, but I can let you know on Monday.'

They became silent once more. The sun beat down, roasting the land in such a heat that even the cicadas sounded drowsy.

When Vives's wife came out with the coffee she found both of them were asleep.

Except on a Sunday, when it often became grossly over-crowded, Parelona beach was still beautiful, a boast which perhaps no other easily accessible beach on the island could make. There was the hotel, set in magnificent colour-scrambled gardens: there were a few villas, but these were owned by the rich who, as always, took great care to shield themselves from the gaze of the common herd and thereby happily ensured that both they and their villas were largely concealed; and there was the ferry pier and café, but these were to the west and could be ignored. Otherwise it was a scene of mountains, pine trees, and cerulean sea. This might have been where Venus was born.

Diana and Waynton were in the centre of the crescent, seated in the shade of one of the straw-covered Tahiti umbrellas set out on the sand and well away from the pine trees and their fallen needles. Between them was a picnic lunch, spread out on a towel.

'He was perfectly nice about it all,' said Waynton, 'but that didn't make his message any pleasanter. It's ten to one Betty *was* murdered, by a man with whom she was having an affair. Even in these permissive days a woman doesn't usually have an affair with a man she doesn't like, so who was she known to be friendly with? That's the point at which I keep returning into the story.'

She picked up a ham roll.

'Can you suggest a candidate other than me?'

'Something has to be wrong in his reasoning,' she said.

'Sure. But what is it?'

'How can I know, Harry?'

'Are you certain you aren't wondering if maybe nothing's wrong after all?'

'Don't be a fool.' But she knew that that tiny doubt had returned like a malignant worm burrowing deep into her mind. For her, all the colour seemed to have been stripped from the scene.

Alvarez walked into the bank and read the poster advising all the bank's customers that if they paid money into their savings accounts within the next month they'd be given tickets for a draw, first prize a house. If he'd been born one of the world's winners, he could have daydreamed about that house.

He spoke to one of the clerks, who was sitting in front of a computer input machine, and the clerk told him to go through to the manager's office. The manager was a round-faced man with thinning hair, horn-rimmed glasses, and a rather severe mouth. He came round and shook hands, rearranged a chair in front of the desk for Alvarez, then returned to his own seat.

'I'd like to know as much as possible about Señor Heron's and Señorita Stevenage's accounts: how much was in them, what kind of total they maintained, and how the money was paid in.'

'Is it true what I've heard – that possibly she was murdered after all?'

'It looks that way at the moment, yes.'

The manager pursed his mouth and shook his head. He stood up and left the room, returning within a minute with a folder. He sat, opened the folder and read, then looked up. 'Señor Heron had a joint account with Señorita Stevenage. Once a month they paid into this account thirty thousand pesetas. When Señor Heron died, the señorita withdrew seventeen thousand pesetas to leave a balance of just over one thousand. This was paid into a new account, in her own name. When she died there was a balance of three thousand two hundred and fifty-three pesetas.'

'This thirty thousand each month – how was that paid in?'

'In cash.'

'How d'you mean – in English notes?'

'In pesetas.'

Alvarez thought about that. 'Isn't it a bit unusual that they paid in pesetas since neither of them had a job here?'

'With all the currency regulations there are in force all over the world and with everyone trying to evade them, I always say that the unusual has become normal.'

'But surely most foreign residents pay in foreign cheques or bank drafts?'

'Yes, they do.'

'Then can you think of any other foreigner who regularly pays pesetas into his account?'

'Some clients have their main account with one bank and use ours just for day-to-day expenses so they pay peseta cheques in to us to give themselves a running credit. Although I can't think of anyone who regularly pays in cash under the same principle, it's obviously perfectly feasible.'

Alvarez sighed. 'I suppose I'll have to check every bank to find out whether they did have their main accounts somewhere else. But it still seems a bit screwy to move the money in cash instead of by cheque. Thirty thousand would be a hell of a lot to lose or have pinched.'

'For some foreigners it would merely be like you or me losing a handful of small change.'

That was what being wealthy meant, thought Alvarez: you could lose a fortune and yet not think about committing suicide.

The calls from the last of the many banks on the island came through at seven thirty-four on Tuesday evening. Alvarez was in his office, dejectedly trying to complete some paperwork which had been due back at HQ a month before.

'We've never held any account in either the name of William Heron or Elizabeth or Betty Stevenage,' said a pleasant-sounding woman. 'That goes for all our branches.'

'I see. Well, thanks a lot.'

'That's all right. I hope it's helped.'

Helped? he thought, as he replaced the receiver. He was damned if he knew whether it had or hadn't. He'd made certain that the monthly sum of thirty thousand hadn't come from any other form of deposit or savings account and now he knew it hadn't come from a bank. So where in the hell had it come from?

CHAPTER XXIII

Denise had been told by her mother, just after she'd met Rodriguez Roldán, that there had been Arab blood on her father's side of the family. She hadn't been certain whether this was a typically convoluted criticism of Roldán or a sign that her mother had been drinking more heavily than usual: she hadn't even known whether it was true – her father had died when she was only twelve and he had never spoken to her about his family. But there were times when she liked to think it was true because for her it accounted for the intensity of her emotions. When she was asked to her first dance, she had been so excited she had been physically sick: the first time she had been kissed with passion, she'd heard a heavenly chorus: she could have killed the first man who made it very clear that all his words of love were meant to be no more than a prelude to action. Other women, she knew, were saddened by tragedy and excited by love, but always at a less intense level than she . . . They didn't have Arab blood in them.

She'd saved for a year and managed to hide the money from her mother and then she and Jacqueline had gone on a package tour to Mallorca. Because, by chance, they'd chosen a hotel in Puerto Llueso, they'd arrived to find a beauty which had immediately captivated her as completely as the ugliness of one of the many concrete jungles on the island would have appalled her.

On the second evening, Jacqueline had met a man who looked and acted like a waiter off duty but who claimed to be a wealthy landowner. She hadn't believed him, but he was fun and so she went out with him. On the fourth evening, Denise had met Roldán and she had fallen in love.

She was not a fool and so she could (thanks to her Arab blood) see him as her knight in shining armour, yet (thanks to her French blood) recognize that he was far from perfect. He was far too vain over his appearance. He valued the material things in life and had little time for the spiritual ones: he judged others more by their wealth than their characters. He was a doctor and therefore should have been dedicated to helping the sick irrespective of their background, yet if two people lay ill he would always choose to minister to the rich one first.

They had married less than a year after their first meeting and had gone to Portugal for their honeymoon. During this fortnight, Roldán had at last begun to realize the quality of the woman he had married. And it was to his credit that he had from then on seen the marriage more in the light of a partnership than a dictatorship – an unusual attitude for a Mallorquin husband to adopt.

Because Denise was both emotional dreamer and yet practical, the marriage had become what she believed the majority of marriages were, a lasting experience of deep and complete love. There were rows, since they both had quick tempers, but these never lasted for long and in any case they were always eager for the sweet satisfaction of reconciliation.

She had always had good taste, although it could have been claimed with some justification that she was too impulsively adventurous at times, and so since her husband was earning a good income she had dressed well and had had their house decorated and furnished with some extravagance: an extravagance which had increased in the recent past as her love of antiques grew. The Mallorquins had never spent much on either themselves or their homes – either because there had been so little money around or because they refused to 'waste' it – so they had watched with contempt (and jealousy) the way in which Roldán and his foreign wife squandered their money. To her astonishment, Denise discovered that she had less contact with the islanders the longer she lived among them. When she thought about this it saddened her, but she didn't think about it very often. She had a husband whom she loved beyond description and who loved her equally. Therefore, nothing else really mattered. Her Arabic ancestors had been very kind to her.

The carriage clock, made in France but bought in Palma, struck eleven o'clock. Denise yawned. 'I'm for bed. How about you?'

Roldán, now wearing a silk shirt and grey flannels, just went on reading a medical journal.

She stood up. 'Did I remember to tell you that Emilio and Rosa have asked us to dinner on Saturday?'

'Tomorrow?' he asked shortly.

'Is tomorrow Saturday? No, it can't be for then so it must be Saturday week.'

'Can't you ever get anything right the first time?'

She looked at him, wondering again what was worrying him so much. For some days now he'd obviously been under considerable strain, yet when she'd tried to talk to him about it he had refused to discuss the matter.

She spoke gaily, as if she'd noticed nothing. 'Ricky, when I was in Palma this afternoon I saw a shop in the Borne with a most beautiful ivory fan. It was hand painted and the outside plates were chased silver.'

He finally looked up. 'How much was it?'

'Only thirty thousand and I bet they'd come down five

thousand if one bargained.'

He was about to say they couldn't afford it because they'd been spending so much recently, but then he saw the expression on her face. He nodded. She rushed across and kissed him.

'You are wonderful! I'll put it in my case of nick-nacks, on the second shelf. When it's spread out, it'll look absolutely lovely . . . Or maybe I'll change things round a bit first.'

'Again?'

She laughed. 'Half the fun of having a collection is to keep moving everything around. It makes all the pieces so much more alive. Come on through to the other room and let's try altering things a bit now. Maybe you'll have one of your brainwaves.'

'I thought you were tired and were off to bed?'

'I've woken up.'

He shook his head. 'I must finish this article.'

'You're getting far too serious, Ricky. It's time you took me dancing, so let's go out tomorrow evening?'

'If we don't discover we're meant to be somewhere you've forgotten all about.'

'Stop acting so superior. You'd get everything totally confused if it weren't for your precious Vestal Virgin. D'you think she really is so belligerently pure as she looks?'

'You've asked me that over and over again and every time I give you the same answer: I don't know.'

The phone rang.

'Blast!' she exclaimed. 'Look at the time. If that's a patient, I'll tell 'em to wait until tomorrow morning before becoming sick.'

'It's all right, I'll go and get the call.' He dropped the magazine on to the floor.

'Stay right where you are. I know you. You'll agree to rush out if it's just some old biddy with a bit of a headache. If I answer the call I can find out if anything's really wrong.'

He watched her leave the room. Since he had married her, he had not bedded another woman. That was the measure of his love for her.

The nearest telephone was in the room which the receptionist – the Vestal Virgin – used as an office. Denise entered and crossed to the small desk. She lifted the receiver. 'Doctor Roldán's house.'

A man, his voice strained, said hoarsely in English: 'There's been an awful accident. My wife's bleeding terribly. The doctor's got to come immediately. Ca'n Asped in the Llueso urbanizacion.'

Denise, to help her husband, had learned English. 'Please, what kind of accident – ' But as she spoke the connection was cut.

She returned to the sitting-room. 'It was for you, darling, and not a headache this time. A man who lives in Ca'n Asped in the Llueso urbanizacion says his wife's had a bad accident and is bleeding seriously.'

'What's his name?'

'He never gave it. I tried to get some details, but he was in such a state he just rang off.'

He hurried into the hall, where he always kept his black pigskin case. As he picked this up, he called out: 'If the woman needs an injection, Sister Teresa's on duty tonight.' As a doctor, he did not give injections. 'If it's emergency surgery, I'll ring you to get the room ready.'

He left the house, backed his car out of the garage, and drove through the narrow streets to the main Palma–Puerto road. At the traffic islands he went straight across and then up the road past the football pitch.

At the first cross-roads within the urbanizacion there were a number of signboards, bearing the names of houses and arrows to indicate in which direction those houses lay. He slowed right down and in the light of the headlights saw that Ca'n Asped was to the left.

The road rose steeply and at the T junction, where he had to turn right, he dropped down to first gear. He accelerated fiercely after the turn, up the road which zig-zagged its way up the side of the mountain. The views from here were dramatic and the costs of building very high – only the rich lived in this area, he thought, with quiet satisfaction.

The road made a hairpin left-hand turn, so sharp that he only just managed to get round in one lock, then rose still more precipitously. Holidaymakers' homes, he thought: access was too difficult for a resident. The woman might well bleed to death because either she or her husband had wanted to live with a view.

There was a large house, set below the level of the road on the left-hand side, and even at night it was possible to judge the amount of work which had been involved merely to blast out level space for the foundations. There was enough moonlight for him to be able to make out a swimming pool, which must have had to be built up at least a couple of metres. Money had obviously been no object.

The drive led off the road, but when he turned into this he found a raised chain drawn across the track to prevent access. He swore. Why in the hell hadn't the husband had the sense to come out and take the chain down? And why weren't there any outside lights on to help him? He picked up a torch as well as his bag, left the car, and walked down the drive, steep enough to make him careful of his balance.

He hammered on the panelled front door. The seconds

passed and nothing happened. He tried the handle, but
the door was locked. Could this be the wrong house? But
no sooner had he asked himself this than he saw, in the
torchlight, a glazed stone set in the wall to the right of the
door on which was the name Ca'n Asped. Then, tragically,
were there two Ca'n Aspeds in the urbanizacion? He
hammered again, much more violently.

The house remained silent and blacked out. He hurried
to his left, passing the garage, and came to the edge of
the levelled area, guarded by a low wall. From here he
could see that there were no lights on in any of the rooms
on that side of the house.

If a mistake had been made – either by the man who
had phoned or by Denise – then a woman might be dying.
But in truth was there no emergency and had someone
been playing a practical joke? Some of the locals were
stupid enough, and envious enough . . . But wouldn't
Denise have noticed the accented English . . .?

It was now virtually impossible to believe this house was
occupied and there had been a serious accident in it.
Nevertheless he hammered on the front door for a third
time in case the husband had panicked into stupidity.
When there was still no movement, he returned to his car.
How to discover whether there was another Ca'n Asped in
the urbanizacion? Or how to identify the bloody fool of a
practical joker?

He started the engine, backed on to the road, and went
down, accelerating hard, venting some of his anger and
frustration by driving even faster than he usually did. He
remembered on the way up passing a house which had
been ablaze with lights and in front of which had been
parked half a dozen cars – he could ask there if anyone
knew of a second Ca'n Asped.

He braked for the very sharp hairpin bend and the

pedal went straight down to the floor. For a part of a second he disbelieved his own senses, as the engine note rose on the over-run, then he pumped the pedal up and down. The brakes still failed to work. He tried to change down to first to use the lower gear as a brake, but when he went to slam the gear lever home he discovered that now the car was going too fast. He wrenched the wheel over to ram the rock face, but he had left it too late. The tail came round in a vicious skid and he tried to correct the skid with opposite lock, but this lurched him over to the outside of the bend.

As the car went over the unguarded edge and began the first of a series of sickening roll-overs, he thought of Denise. He hadn't fixed his safety-belt and was thrown sideways, to feel pain begin to spear his side. Then the car upended and he was thrown against the windscreen and steering-wheel, losing consciousness immediately.

CHAPTER XXIV

In his office, Alvarez read the Telex message which had just been brought to him: 'Originator, Detective Inspector Fletcher. Eighth July, eleven hundred hours. Probate Monica Heron granted sixteenth October, confirm two hundred and fifty-three thousand four hundred and sixteen pounds fifty-three pence. All accounts belonging Heron emptied October twentieth. Nothing more known.'

Two hundred and fifty-three thousand pounds (unlike Fletcher, he found it much easier to round off the figure) which had virtually disappeared.

He heaved himself to his feet and crossed to the very old and battered filing cabinet. In one of the drawers there should be a parcel with all the papers which had been found in Ca'n Ibore after the death of Señorita Stevenage. He checked through the muddle, eventually found what he wanted, and returned to the desk.

Bills, receipts, a cash book, a cheque book and several books of cheque stubs, bank statements . . . But no letters, address book, diary, or any papers of a purely personal nature.

He read through the bank statements and the cheque stubs. The picture was exactly as the bank manager had presented it. Thirty thousand pesetas paid into, and about thirty thousand withdrawn from, the account each month. So where was the two hundred and fifty-three thousand and all the interest this must be making? In an account in another country? Surely some reference to that account would have been left behind by Heron, but there was no reference among these papers. Yet after the death of

Heron, Betty Stevenage had paid into her own account (the one she had opened after emptying the joint account) one sum of thirty thousand pesetas, so she must have known of a source of money which she could tap. And where did the thirty thousand regularly turn up from, when it had been shown that it had never come through any of the normal sources of cash? Neither Heron nor the señorita had left the island from the day they arrived . . .

He sighed, looked at his watch, and was slightly comforted to discover that it was almost time for lunch.

When he arrived home, Dolores was laying the table. 'You're better than an alarm clock, Enrique.' She put a kilo loaf of bread on a board down on the table.

'My uncle always told me, eat regularly and you'll live to be old.'

'Was that your Uncle Miguel? From all accounts he knew more about drinking regularly than eating regularly.'

'Maybe. But he did live to be ninety-one. Though God knows if in the end he thought it worth the bother.'

She turned and stared at him, her dark eyes suddenly filled with concern. 'What's the matter with you today?'

'I'm sick: sick of having a mind which goes round and round in circles and ends up by tripping over its own tail. There are times when I wish I'd refused to go to Damián's and Teresa's wedding.'

She put her hands on her hips. 'What the hell are you on about? Have you been boozing?'

'Not a drop all morning. Cross my heart and hope to die.'

'Don't take the risk.'

He slumped down in a chair. 'If I hadn't gone to the wedding I wouldn't have listened to Francisca and then life would have been so much simpler. Francisca talks far too much.'

'Just because you're out of sorts . . . She's a wonderful cook and keeps that house of hers as clean as a new pin . . .'

He ceased to listen to a long list of Francisca's virtues: when a woman talked too much nothing could compensate for that fact.

Jaime, Juan and Isabel came into the house together and the two children were having a shouted argument. Alvarez loved his family because it gave him an identity.

They had started the first course – a thick fish soup – when Dolores said: 'I suppose you've heard about that dreadful accident last night?'

'What accident?' asked Alvarez.

'I'd have thought someone would have told you! Dr Roldán was killed in a car smash last night.'

'Sweet Mary!' said Jaime automatically.

'Rodriguez Roldán?' asked Alvarez.

'The doctor who's always dressed up like a tailor's dummy and is married to that Frenchwoman who puts on such airs and graces.'

'He's always driven around like a maniac,' said Jaime, 'so it's no wonder he's had a smash. What happened?'

'Margarita said he was up in the urbanizacion visiting a patient and drove right over the edge of the road. The car rolled over and over and he was crushed to death.'

How long ago was it, thought Alvarez, that he had called at Roldán's house and had so envied him? Now he was dead and his wife was a widow . . . A man left his house a thousand times and returned a thousand times, then left it once more and did not return . . .

Alvarez could not sleep: every time he was about to drop off his mind suddenly became so active it jerked him awake once more. Finally he gave up the struggle, sat upright, rubbed his eyes, and then stood up and went round the desk to the window to open the shutters. The nearby church clock struck four. Moodily he stared down at the empty street which shimmered in the heat.

He could not forget the way Roldán's wife had looked at Roldán that evening, only a week ago. Then, they had been two of the luckiest people in the world. Yet now . . . Feeling old and sad, he returned to the desk and used the internal phone to speak to the traffic section.

'Yeah, the doc bought it last night, all right,' said the man at the other end of the line. 'He went straight off the road and by the time he reached the bottom he was flatter than a pancake.'

'Was he tight?'

'His wife says he'd had no more than one drink before the meal and a glass of wine with the meal. And from all accounts he wasn't a real drinking man. The tests'll tell us for sure, but at the moment it's ten to one he was sober.'

'Then why did he go over the edge?'

'There was a phone call to go to Ca'n Asped double quick sharp because a woman had had a very serious accident and her husband said she was bleeding badly. Roldán drove to the house, which is right up the urbanizacion where the road aims pretty near straight for the sky. When he left he must have been going at a rate of knots and right now it looks like brake failure, because there aren't any rubber marks on the road until almost at the bend where he obviously tried to turn in to the rock face and only succeeded in skidding over the edge.'

'Was it an old car?'

'Practically brand new Seat one-three-one.'

'Hasn't that got a dual braking system?'

'I wouldn't know off-hand.'

'What about the people he called on – can they help at all?'

'There wasn't anyone in the house: been shut up for the past nine months. The owners live in England and only come out for the last part of July and whole of August and sometimes Christmas. Either Roldán's wife got the address wrong or it was a hoax.'

'A hoax?'

'I know. That sounds pretty thin to me too.'

'If Señora Roldán got the name wrong, wouldn't he have realized this from the name of the patient?'

'As far as I know, no name was ever given, only the address, and since they would have been new patients Roldán hadn't any way of checking. But the wife's in such a state it's difficult to get any sense out of her.'

'Is the car being checked over?'

'Of course. How come you're this interested, Enrique?'

'I don't know, really. Maybe it's because I was speaking to the man only a week ago.'

'Here today, gone tomorrow. That's the way the world goes. So drink and wench while you still can.'

After the call was over, Alvarez stared at the far wall. Roldán had been Heron's doctor, but so had he been the doctor of hundreds of other people. Heron's wife had died from accidental poisoning. Betty Stevenage's dog had been poisoned with aconite and probably it was aconite which had killed her. Surely it could be only one more coincidence that Roldán's name was linked with theirs . . .?

CHAPTER XXV

On Monday, a day promising to be even hotter than before, Alvarez walked throvgh the town to the Seat garage. The wrecked car was on a low trolley in a corner bay. It was so shattered and twisted that without very close inspection it was impossible to judge that it had been a Seat 131.

He went over to where Largo, the owner of the garage, was working on the prop shaft of a six-metre speedboat in a cradle. 'Have you checked out the crashed car yet?'

Largo, a short, stocky man with a humorous face, straightened up and pressed a clenched fist against the small of his back. 'Not yet. They brought it in yesterday and I had to open up the garage specially to take it. This morning I've this boat to repair: the owner wanted it days ago.'

'So when d'you think you'll get round to the car?'

'When I've the time.'

'It's important.'

'So are the paying customers.'

Alvarez leaned against the hull of the speedboat. 'You've looked over enough wrecked cars in your time, Alberto. D'you reckon you'll be able to judge what caused the accident?'

'With a car as bashed up as that? When they brought it in I told 'em, you're wasting your time and mine. But they insisted – check over the remains and tell us why the car went over the edge.'

'Traffic seems to think the brakes must have failed.'

'All right. You check the brake lines and tell me if they

were damaged before or after the crash. You tell me if the reservoirs of brake fluid were empty before he went over.'

'OK, OK. I take your point.'

'Have a fag,' said Largo, producing a pack from his oil-stained overalls, 'and forget it. Worry only gives you ulcers.'

'I reckon I must be growing a champion crop,' said Alvarez gloomily.

Alvarez stood by the entrance to the drive to Ca'n Asped and looked upwards. The road turned in a right-hand hairpin bend fifty metres on. He looked downwards. A three-hundred-metre run down a very steep road. If Roldán had been very annoyed by the abortive call he might well have driven off with reckless speed . . .

He walked downhill. There was no form of barrier on the outer edge of the road, but the very obviousness of the danger surely was a safety measure? At night time, any driver who wasn't either drunk or mad would stick to the centre of the road. Where was the last point at which one would normally brake? He judged the point would be opposite a ledge of rock, left after the road had been blasted out, on which grew a solitary spurge bush. Reaction to brake failure might be quick, but it couldn't be instantaneous and the car would travel quite a few metres before the driver's brain realized the brakes had gone and he reacted to this knowledge. Then an attempt to drop down into a lower gear? And the last, desperate act, to try to ram the rock to bring the car to a stop? . . . The road was marked with black rubber strips where the Seat had skidded . . . He reached the edge of the road and looked down and immediately suffered the nausea which heights always produced in him. Exercising considerable will-power, and courage, he forced himself to stand still and study the scene. The mountainside sloped away unevenly, its surface a jumble of levels, with bushes and scrub grass growing in sparse pockets. The passage of the car could readily be traced out: gouged rock, smashed bushes whose leaves were already brown, shattered glass which glinted in the sunlight and jagged pieces of metal.

To him, the scene suggested only one thing, brake failure. Yet the car had a dual braking system and the odds against both systems failing together were surely very, very great?

He began to climb up the road and soon the sweat was rolling down his face, neck, and back, and he was having to breathe through opened mouth.

Alvarez had never been able dispassionately to observe another's grief: he was far too emotional for that. So to an extent Denise Roldán's tragedy became a tragedy for him.

'Señora, I am desperately sorry to have to bother you at such a terrible time.'

She said nothing. She was dressed in black and by some terrible irony black so suited her that she looked more beautifully elegant than ever – only her eyes betrayed the depths of her misery.

'I have to question you about the telephone call on Friday night.'

She had a lace-edged handkerchief in her lap and she plucked at this with the fingers of her right hand.

'I believe that you answered the call?'

She nodded.

'Can you remember exactly how it went?'

Staring straight in front of herself, she said tonelessly: 'The man said his wife had had a terrible accident and was bleeding very badly. The doctor was to come immediately to Ca'n Asped in the Llueso urbanizacion.'

'What language did he speak?'

'English.'

'Do you think he was English?'

'Yes.'

'Do you understand the language well?'

'I've learned it to be able to help Ricky. He needs . . .' She stopped as she realized that the present tense was no longer applicable.

'Would you say you understood English well enough not to make a mistake in translating it either to yourself or someone else?'

A few tears had spilled out of her eyes and run down her cheeks. She brushed them away with her hand. 'Yes.'

'Did the man tell you his name?'

'No. I asked him for it, but he rang off.'

'Señora, please bear with my questions, but do you think you could possibly have been mistaken over the name of the house?'

She turned and stared straight at him, yet he was certain she was not really seeing him. 'D'you think I haven't been asking myself over and over again, did I make a mistake? If Ricky had gone to another house, he would be alive now. So if I heard wrongly, I killed him. But the man said Ca'n Asped. I swear it.'

'Did you recognize his voice, señora?'

'No.'

'Do you know many of the English residents?'

She shook her head.

He stood up and thanked her. She gave no sign that she had heard him.

Alvarez entered the town hall, a large, rather church-like building, and walked along a narrow, badly-lit passage to a room which was largely filled with filing cabinets and dusty ledgers.

A small man, very dark complexioned, was searching amongst the ledgers and sneezing at irregular intervals.

'I need some help,' said Alvarez.

'We're terribly busy . . .'

'It won't take you long. Just draw up a list of all the houses called Ca'n Asped and any name which is pretty similar which are in any of the local urbanizacions.'

'But that'll take hours and hours,' said the clerk plaintively. He was about to say something more when the beginning of a sneeze robbed him of the powers of speech.

Alvarez took off his spectacles, which he should have worn far more often than he did, and rubbed his nose. There was only the one house called Ca'n Asped and there was no house with a name so similar that it was reasonable to suppose Señora Roldán could have confused the one with the other. He recalled the gist of the telephone conversation. A woman gravely injured and bleeding badly. If the call had been genuine, then there had been a husband who must have become quite frantic when Roldán failed to turn up. Clearly, he would have telephoned another doctor . . . Alvarez telephoned all the doctors who lived in Llueso and Puerto Llueso and none of them had attended an Englishwoman who had been badly injured on Friday night.

Had the call been a very stupid practical joke? It didn't seem reasonable to believe any of the English community would have played such a joke because the Roldáns apparently knew none of them well. A Mallorquin, filled with spite, might have been responsible, except that Denise Roldán was certain the caller had been English –

and over the telephone any accent usually became magnified. Then the call had been made in order to get Roldán's car up on a dangerous road where it could be sabotaged, so that when he left he was driving to his death. Why? Because he knew, or suspected, the identity of the murderer of Señorita Stevenage?

He stood up and wandered over to the window. If he did nothing and allowed the apparent accident to remain an accident, then a brutal murderer might escape, perhaps to murder yet again: but if he pursued what he now believed to be the truth, he must cause Denise Roldán even greater misery because he would be blackening the character of her husband. He sighed.

He left the office, went down to his car, and drove the short distance to Roldán's house.

Roldán's mother, a frail woman of eighty who opened the door, lamented and wept as Alvarez murmured words of condolence: for her, grief needed to be expressed openly. But for Denise grief was a very private matter, and at first when she spoke to Alvarez in the main sitting-room she was as coldly self-controlled as she had been before, when her emotions had to some extent been anaesthetized by the initial shock.

'Señora, I'm very sorry, but I must ask you some more questions about your husband.' He paused, then continued more quickly: 'You see, now I am not certain it was an accident.'

'What do you mean?'

'It's possible the accident was deliberate.'

'Mother of God!' she whispered. 'Someone murdered him?'

'There's no other house called Ca'n Asped, or any name which could be mistaken for that one. And I've checked and no other doctor in the area was called out to attend a badly injured woman. If there had been a badly bleeding wife, the husband must have tried to call help from another doctor when Doctor Roldán failed to turn up.'

'Who would kill him?' Her voice was little more than a whisper.

'Señora, it is possible . . .' After a brief pause, he doggedly continued. 'It is possible that your husband knew the identity of the man who murdered Señorita Stevenage. And because he knew, he had to be killed to prevent his saying who that man was.'

She murmured something he failed to catch.

'I will have to examine what drugs he has been using and also speak to the receptionist. And perhaps look through his accounts.'

'Why?'

'Because it is possible that he sold some poison to someone.'

It took her a little time to understand the full inference of his words, but when she did she shouted wildly at him and although she had been shouting in French he knew she was cursing him for his vile suspicions. Her mother-in-law ran into the room and, without understanding the reason for the turmoil, began to wail as she drew Denise to her to comfort her.

He left, hating himself, his job, and a world in which one person could be so terribly hurt.

CHAPTER XXVI

Carolina Belderrain – the Vestal Virgin about whom Denise had so often teased her husband – was a woman in her early forties whose face had the misfortune to appear to be out of proportion no matter from which direction it was observed. Even her beautiful eyes, deep, warm brown, were too large in relation to her high forehead so that they appeared constantly to be expressing astonishment.

Her manner was defensively abrupt, even antagonistic: Roldán's unpopularity with many Mallorquins had, in fact, been partially due to her. 'No,' she snapped, 'it's quite impossible.'

Alvarez looked across the sitting-room of her house, a room filled to overflowing with furniture, a collection of china figurines, and four garishly coloured paintings. 'Señorita, I think that nothing is completely impossible.'

'You don't know what you're talking about: suggesting the doctor would ever have sold poison to someone. It's completely disgusting.'

'There's reason for thinking . . .'

'Don't they teach you people anything? Doctors work to save lives, not take them.'

'Unfortunately, it's not every doctor who remembers that.'

'Well, Doctor Roldán did. Oh, don't think I don't know what mean and spiteful things some people used to say about him!' Her scorn increased. 'Just because he dressed really smartly and his wife was beautiful and because he wouldn't live in a slum like them. But he was a different kind of a person.'

He wondered whether she saw herself as a different kind of a person.

'They resented his success. They couldn't understand why he didn't hoard his money under a loose floorboard, but spent it all on enjoying himself: they couldn't understand why he was always ready to accept new ideas, instead of rejecting them out of hand. He once said to me . . .' She stopped.

'Yes, señorita?'

She shook her head, as if marvelling over something. 'He once said to me, "When I started practising medicine, I saw myself setting out on a crusade. But now I know I've just been engaged in muddy trench warfare." '

'Did you understand what he meant by that?'

'Of course. He became a doctor in order to help his own people live better and happier lives. But they were too traditional and stupid to let him. If he wanted to make more than one visit or prescribe more than a couple of aspirins, they said he was just trying to make money out of them.'

'He was once an idealist?'

'He was always an idealist – which is why it's disgustingly absurd to suggest he would have sold anyone poison.'

'If he was an idealist, he was one who liked the good things in life?'

'Who says an idealist has to starve in a garret?'

'I gather that if the poor peasants were suspicious of him, the rich foreigners weren't?'

Her manner became less certain, as if this was a point which in the past had troubled her. 'If the locals were so stupid and suspicious, why shouldn't he tend the foreigners? And why shouldn't they pay for his being a really good doctor? But don't you forget the rest of the story. If someone not very well off wanted him, but their insurance didn't have him on their list, he charged them nothing. And if the medicines were very expensive, he'd pay for them out of his own pocket. That's the kind of man he really was.'

Hadn't someone once said that no man was a hero to his valet? Perhaps no doctor was a villain to his receptionist. And yet although it would be absurd to accept as gospel everything she said – wasn't there too stark a contradiction between the idealist and the doctor who preferred to attend the wealthy foreigner? – he felt that there was some truth in her words. Yet if that were so, surely Roldán would not have given or sold poison to another person, knowing it could be used for only one purpose? And if he had not, why had he been murdered? Yet if he had not been murdered, what had happened to the badly injured Englishwoman . . .?

'Is there any aconite among the medical supplies at the doctor's house?' he asked.

'No,' she replied immediately.

'How can you be quite so certain?'

'The doctor would never keep any poison in the house.'

'Used in very small doses it has therapeutic qualities: I believe it's good for gout.'

'He refused to keep any poison at all because he was scared of there being a dreadful accident. He said it was a chemist's job to keep that sort of thing.'

'I'm sure you're right, but we'd better go along and check his stocks.'

'I am not a liar,' she said with haughty anger.

They drove in his car to Roldán's house. The door was opened by the daily woman who tried to make conversation, but she was brusquely cut short by Carolina: it was obvious that the two women disliked each other.

Carolina led the way into her office and pointed to a

large cupboard. 'All the medicines in the house are in there, except for anything which has to be kept refrigerated.' She opened her handbag and brought out a key. 'There you are.' She all but flung it at him.

The search did not take long because the cupboard was only half-full. There was no aconite, either in extract or in liniment form.

'Do you keep a book listing all medicines in and out?' he asked.

'Of course,' she snapped. She made no move to get this book until he specifically asked her for it.

With her help when this was necessary, very grudgingly given, he checked through all the entries over the past year. No aconite in any form had been purchased during that time.

Alvarez went into the chemist in the Calle Aragon and spoke to the young woman behind the counter and said he'd like a word with the señora. She walked between two of the stock shelves to the rear of the shop, where there were stairs, and shouted: 'Rosalía.'

A woman carrying a small baby in her arms came down the stairs. When she saw Alvarez, she smiled a welcome. He asked how the baby was and it was almost five minutes later before he was able to say: 'D'you remember being questioned about the sale of aconite?'

'Yes, indeed. Not very long ago, was it?'

'No, it wasn't. Well we've been on to every wholesale and retail chemist on the island and everyone's given us the same answer – no aconite. But now something's turned up which suggests there must have been. Now, tell me right off the record. Suppose a doctor you knew personally came in and asked for some poison, only a very little, would you always bother to make a record of that sale?

After all, he's entitled to buy whatever he needs and lots of poisons are used in medicine.'

'We'd bother, whoever it was, for our own sake just as much as for the rules. If there's any trouble over a poison, every single milligram has to be accounted for or we can be in big trouble.'

He rubbed his heavy chin. 'If Doctor Roldán had come in and bought a very small amount of aconite from you, then that purchase would have been entered in the book?'

'It most certainly would.'

'D'you remember his ever coming in and asking about buying some aconite?'

She looked curiously at him. 'No. He's never done that.'

He thanked her and left the shop. Once seated in his car, he lit a cigarette. Almost certainly all the other local chemists would give the same answers as Rosalía had just given him – and as for chemists further afield, Roldán would probably not have been personally known to them so that the regulations would have been strictly complied with and the purchase recorded. So as he had not left the island in the past year, what other source for the poison could he have drawn on? Extracting it from the roots of monkshood? But this was a fairly complicated process apparently, and could he manage to do the work in total secrecy, in a town where everybody's business was everybody else's? Perhaps. But he could not forget Carolina's contemptuous dismissal of the possibility that Roldán could ever have had a hand in poisoning someone.

CHAPTER XXVII

Alvarez looked through the window of the showroom at the white Seat 132.

'You can have it for a third down and three years' HP,' said a voice from his left.

He turned to face Largo, dressed for once not in grease-stained overalls but in an open-necked shirt and well pressed trousers. 'Would anybody be fool enough to give credit to a mere inspector in the Cuerpo General de Policia?'

Largo chuckled. 'Probably not. Maybe we'd both better forget the deal after all.'

'Have you checked over that crashed car yet?'

'We've done the best we can, Enrique, but it's mostly like I said it would be. When a car gets really crumpled up, you can't tell much.'

'You sound as if you might have found something, though?'

'There was what seems to have been a loose union on one of the brake lines. If it was loose, that couldn't have happened in the crash.'

'So was at least one of the systems definitely inoperative?'

'Can't say. It all depends how bad the leak had been – if there was a leak.'

'That's nothing but ifs.'

Largo shrugged his shoulders.

'If that had been a developing fault and all the fluid had drained away, there'd still be braking power left on the other circuit?'

'That's right.'

'On opposite wheels, front and back. So if he'd panic-braked there would have been rubber on the road?'

'Almost certainly.'

'If you knew what you were doing, how long would it take you to immobilize both brake lines?'

'Say half a minute, unless you were going to do it crudely. Then ten seconds would be enough.'

Alvarez visualized the scene on the night of the crash. He 'saw' the doctor climb out of his car and walk down the sloping path to the front door swearing because the chain had prevented his driving all the way down. A shadowy figure came round the bend immediately above the house. As the doctor hammered on the door, wondering why the frantic husband didn't let him in, the man immobilized both brake lines, then returned to the cover of the bend. The doctor, furious and frustrated, drove off at a rate of knots . . . 'Thanks for all your help,' he said.

'Not much we could do for you, I'm afraid. But there it is.'

There was sick, bitter anger etched in Denise Roldán's face. As she sat in the red velvet chair in the sitting-room, which so dramatically set off her black dress, Alvarez could guess what thoughts poured through her mind. Why him? What had he ever done to be singled out by a malign fate? Alvarez remembered the days after the death of Juana-Maria, when his grief had seemed a physical pain and he had resented, instead of welcomed, comforting words. 'Señora, I am very, very sorry to have to return to bother you. But I need to look through the doctor's papers and his bank statements. If this weren't absolutely necessary . . .'

'He couldn't ever have sold poison to anyone. It's a

filthy thing to suggest.' Her voice rose. 'He loved his work. When he came home and told me he'd helped to save a life, had brought relief from pain, or even when all he'd done was to give an innoculation which would maybe prevent a child becoming fatally ill one day, he used to say that he felt he was helping God. He was a religious man. Can't you see what that meant? His work of helping the sick was part of his religion. So how can you believe he would have sold poison that killed?'

Perhaps a man could believe he might serve both God and mammon, despite all the strictures to the contrary. Perhaps Dr Roldán had seen his healing in divine terms, but its rewards in commercial ones. If so, she was right, he could never have sold or given poison to anyone. 'Señora, I can only say again, I am ashamed to have to ask to see his papers, but because of my work I must.'

Her expression became cruelly contemptuous.

'Where did he keep all his papers?'

'In his office.'

'And where is that?'

'Next to the surgery.'

'Has anything been removed from his office?'

'No one has been in it since the night he . . . he . . . God, I hope one day it happens to you,' she said wildly.

'Señora,' he answered sombrely, 'many years ago just such a tragedy happened to me.'

She put her clenched hand to her mouth and began to cry. In between sobs, she whispered: 'Sweet Mary, I'm sorry.'

He went over to her and held her against his side for a moment. 'Señora, words are useless, or I would use a thousand. But gradually help will come through time.'

'I loved him so completely. Perhaps that's why it happened. We loved too much.'

After a while, when her crying had died away, he left. She was right. There was room in the world for every degree of envy, hatred, and brutality, but there was no room for very great love. God was a jealous god.

The office was an oblong room in which were a glass-fronted bookcase, a metal filing cabinet looking incongruous next to a beautifully inlaid roll-top desk, a flat, leather-topped desk with drawers on either side of the well, a leather, adjustable chair, a carpet which he took to be Persian and which was filled with colour, and two paintings on the wall.

Dr Roldán had kept meticulous financial records: there were separate account books for his work and his domestic expenses and cheque stubs and bank statements covering the past five years.

After a while, a pattern became clear. Roldán had enjoyed a considerable income throughout the past five years and for most of that time his expenditure had equalled his income. But suddenly, in March of the present year, he had begun to make purchases, often expensive ones, without either drawing a cheque or the necessary cash. Alvarez added up such amounts and they totalled over two hundred thousand pesetas.

He leaned back in the chair. Two hundred thousand pesetas which were unaccounted for. He remembered Francisca at the wedding of Damián and Teresa telling them how Dr Roldán and his wife had begun to spend money as if it were going out of fashion.

He bundled up the relevant records and put them into half a dozen very large envelopes. He left. She was still in the sitting-room, in the same chair. He sat opposite her. 'In these envelopes I've some papers, bank statements, and cheque stubs, which I must take away with me. I will, of course, give you a receipt for them.'

She was indifferent to what he said.

'Señora, when it came to financial matters, did you work with your husband? Did you both check through accounts?'

'He did all that sort of thing,' she answered dully.

'Were you given a certain amount of money for house-keeping each week?'

'He gave me as much as I needed.'

'In cash?'

'Yes.'

'And when you bought furniture for the house, like that beautiful roll-top desk in the office, how did you pay for it?'

'I can't remember.'

'I know your husband banked at the Llueso branch of the Caja de Ahorros y Monte de Piedad de Las Baleares, but did he bank anywhere else as well?'

'No.'

'Have you a safe in this house?'

She shook her head.

He stood up. 'Thank you for being so kind.'

She looked up. 'D'you understand now? He couldn't have sold poison to anyone.'

Alvarez spoke to the bank manager in his office. 'I want to know if Dr Roldán kept any valuables deposited with you?'

'I'll have to check up on that for you.'

The manager was gone from his room for less than a minute and he brought back with him a large ledger. 'Yes, he did. Deposited a briefcase with us on March 16. He's had it out a few times since, always re-depositing it.'

'D'you know what's in it?'

'I've no idea. We never ask a customer what he deposits, just make it clear that the deposit is made entirely at his own risk.'

'I'd like to see this briefcase.'

The manager said doubtfully: 'This will be part of his estate. I really ought to have some kind of authorization from the family or the solicitors . . .'

'All I want to do is find out what it contains. If you're going to become all sticky about it I'll have to go off and get an official order, which means a great deal more trouble for both of us.'

The manager sighed. 'There's enough trouble around without adding to it . . . All right, I'll get it.'

The pigskin briefcase was a large one, capable of being greatly expanded. It was locked.

'Give me a paperclip, will you?' said Alvarez.

'You're surely not going to force the lock?'

'Well, I haven't got the key.'

'I don't think I can stand here and let you do that, Enrique.'

'Then go away and don't come back until I shout it's all right.'

The manager stayed and watched with fascination as Alvarez first straightened out the paperclip, then bent one end, inserted this end and worked on the lock, forcing it within three minutes.

Alvarez opened the briefcase and looked inside. He saw several bundles of thousand-peseta notes.

CHAPTER XXVIII

Alvarez faced Denise. 'Señora, I have discovered that your husband deposited a briefcase at his bank. In this is a large number of thousand-peseta notes: their total value is seven hundred and sixty-five thousand pesetas.'

She was uninterested.

'Did you know he had all this money?'

She shook her head.

'It's a fair judgement that originally there were a million pesetas. Señora, the money your husband earned was all paid into his bank account. So where did this million come from?'

'I don't know.' She fidgeted with a button on her dress.

'Don't you realize that if I can't find out where it came from I'm bound to start wondering if perhaps he was paid it for providing the poison?'

She looked at him with renewed contempt. 'You can still think he'd sell poison to kill someone? Don't you understand the first thing about another human being?'

'If there are . . .'

'If he'd been offered ten million pesetas his answer would have been the same. Never. And yet you keep on and on asking the same questions, understanding nothing. Oh God, is there nothing left now to prove the kind of man he was? Has he completely disappeared with death?'

He sighed. She had discovered what to the living was the final tragedy of every life, no matter how strong his or her belief. 'The money is being held at the bank, señora, until we can discover its source. If it proves to have been quite legitimately obtained, then of course it will be handed over to the estate.' He stood.

'Who murdered my husband?' she demanded.

He shook his head. 'We can't be certain that he was murdered. If the money in the briefcase . . . If the money is easily explained, then perhaps the car crash was a terrible accident, however we now think. But if your husband kept the money hidden because it was earned illegally, then we can be all but certain that the crash was deliberately engineered.'

'Where did the money come from?'

'But that is what I have been asking you. From somewhere your husband obtained a million pesetas which he kept in a briefcase in his bank. From where or from whom could he have got this money in March?'

She just stared at him.

After a while, he left.

People, Alvarez thought, often talked about facts as if they answered everything: yet there could be facts galore and they could still fail to spell out the story.

How much reliance did one place on a wife's assessment (backed by a receptionist's) of her husband whom she loved totally? A cynic would say that love is notoriously blind. But he couldn't believe that Denise could be totally wrong about her husband's character, even if she could be about his actions. But if that million pesetas hadn't come from the sale of the poison which had been used to murder first the dog and then Betty Stevenage, where had it come from? And why?

It was all beyond a peasant's wits.

CHAPTER XXIX

It was late September and still the weather had not broken as it usually did and the days remained hot and sunny. In the bars, restaurants, and shops down in the Port, the flow of tourists remained high and owners marvelled at their fortune and put up their prices.

Rosalind Jepson's parties were, according to her, social events. Not only was she closely related to a title, she had also married a wealthy husband who, ever an accommodating man, had died quickly and quietly, thus ending a marriage which she had always described as sensible and he, had he ever been asked, would have called bloody cold. She was a composed, stately woman who gave composed, stately parties. It was a measure of the respect and dislike in which she was held that no one ever got really drunk in her house.

Jessica Appleton had dressed with extra care in her very best frock. It was a long, flowing creation in silk which dated from the 'thirties and suggested druidical rights at the summer solstice: a suggestion enhanced by her sharp, rather sour and jaundiced features. She swept out on to the patio, accompanied by a miasma of cheap perfume, and was immediately greeted by a painter who suffered permanently from a bitter, resentful self-pity that Picasso had been born before he had. 'Hullo, Jessica.'

'Hullo, Tom.' She studied the other three who were in the same group. 'Fancy seeing all of you here.'

'You wouldn't,' said the sulky blonde, 'if anyone was giving a better party.'

A maid came up with a tray on which was a bowl of

garlic and cheese dip and a large number of bread sticks.
They helped themselves very generously.

'Jessica, darling,' said the man with a profile, 'tell me
what's been happening in Llueso. I always rely on you to
keep me *au fait* with all the news which no one will print.'

Jessica simpered. 'Well, I did hear something rather
interesting this morning.'

'Good! Good!'

'Hugh's given up his flat and left the island.'

'I don't call that interesting,' said the blonde. She
yawned. 'He said time after time he wasn't going to spend
the rest of his life on this piddling little island.'

'But it's who's gone with him that makes it interesting,'
said Jessica triumphantly. 'Denise.'

'Who?' asked the brunette.

'Denise Roldán. She was the wife of the doctor who was
killed in that terrible car accident up in the urbanizacion.
Just imagine, going off like that so soon after her husband's
death!'

'Darling,' said the man with the profile, 'don't you
think that now you're being just a teeny-weeny bit
suburban?'

Waynton, on the settee in Diana's house, stared out
through the picture window at the distant, mountain-
ringed bay. How much was he going to miss the beauty,
the sun-splashed colours, the lazy air of peace?

Diana returned to the room. 'Sorry to have left you for
so long, but I had to put a load of washing in the machine
or I'd have had nothing to wear tomorrow.'

He watched her sit. 'I've heard a piece of news which
may interest you.'

'News – or malicious gossip?'

'I've checked up on it. Hugh's left the island and pretty

clearly doesn't intend to return.' He watched her face for signs of regret.

'He always said he wouldn't stay.' She appeared to accept the news without any definite emotion.

'He didn't go on his own. Denise Roldán, the widow of the doctor who was killed in the car crash, went with him.'

'Good God! . . . Although maybe I shouldn't be surprised since I saw them together in the town more than once. She looked rather nice.'

'Is that all?'

'What more do you expect me to say?'

'I don't expect you to say anything. It's just that . . . Well, I've never been absolutely certain how much you liked him.'

'He was great fun and when I was with him life was always bubbly. But things never moved on from there.'

'I wondered . . . Di, I'm going back home soon. I reckon I've been rehabilitated out here: people are beginning to speak to me again.'

'Of course. Even the stupidest of them has finally realized that if you had been guilty of murdering Betty, you'd have been arrested by now.'

'It must have been very disappointing for them.'

'Their grief will have been short-lived. The gin and the brandy don't leave much room for long-term emotions.'

He suddenly stood up and crossed to the window. 'I was thinking about how much I'm going to miss everything here when I go back.'

'So are you having second thoughts on that score?'

'No. It's been fun drifting with the wind, but I've got to rejoin life. I just hope it's not going to be too painful.'

'Not for you, Harry – you've always really been out of place here. This island is home for the retired or the spineless. You're far too much of a fighter for it.'

He turned away from the window and faced her. 'I've no job waiting for me.'

'You'll find one soon enough.'

'I've nothing in the bank.'

'Who has, other than overdrafts?'

'But, suffering from all these disadvantages, will you marry me?'

She began to finger her wedding-ring, twisting it round on her finger. 'As it's a day for confessions, I'd better make a few. When I told you I'd hand back all the money my husband settled on me if I married again, I meant exactly that. So I won't own a house or have a large private income and my only capital will be a few hundred pounds an elderly aunt left me. But speaking as one of the new poor, why in the hell has it taken you so long to ask me for the second time?'

Women. Were they born to deceive or did they learn deceit at their mothers' knees? How could Denise Roldán have so betrayed the memory of her love for her husband? Alvarez felt a bitter disillusionment. He had placed her on a pedestal and she had kicked that pedestal over and run away, skirts held high.

He remembered so clearly how she had looked at Roldán. A lie? He remembered her tearing grief over his death. A lie? Was she a consummate actress, able to summon up any emotion at will?

Had she known Roldán was to die? Was there here much deeper and dirtier streams than he had imagined? Had she loved the English señor from their first meeting and had they plotted to rid themselves of the man who stood between them?

He crashed his clenched fist down on the desk. Fool! To believe that even the finest actress ever born could have simulated the love that Denise had shown for her husband ... Yet if she had loved so deeply, how could such love have been destroyed and replaced within a mere two months?

And suddenly, shockingly, he remembered that love had the opposite, dark face of hate. And when one had loved intensely, then one would hate intensely – so intensely that no sacrifice would be too great in the name of revenge.

CHAPTER XXX

Alvarez walked up the dirt track on which cinders had from time to time been spread to try to stiffen the surface when the rains came. He saw almond, fig, orange, lemon, pear, and algarroba trees, beneath which grew potatoes, peppers, beans. He saw a well with a bucket and chain, worked from a spindle, the only source of raising water since electricity had not been brought to the land. He saw the small caseta, made from blocks of sandstone which had been weathered from honey-colour to mottled greys: there was no glass in the windows, only solid wooden shutters, now shut as if no stray beam of sunshine must be allowed to enter. He saw to the side of the caseta a lean-to in which several chickens scratched among the dust and a chained goat nibbled at some stalks. Time could have slipped back fifty years. This was how families had lived when a man's wages were five pesetas a day and he was lucky to work four days in seven.

A woman, old and leathery, her head half lost inside a very wide-brimmed straw hat, was drawing out irrigation channels with a mattock. When he spoke to her she straightened up slowly, as if this action needed great care, and then she stared at him with tired, but stubbornly independent watchfulness. When he asked her where her husband was, she nodded at the house, but gave no other answer.

The caseta's interior was as simple as its exterior. There was a centre room, in one corner of which was a fireplace, and leading off this were a kitchen and a bedroom, both much smaller. The walls and the floors, made from pebbles on end, were scrupulously clean.

Gomez was sitting up in bed, his back propped up by a bare pillow. It seemed he was content to do nothing because the bottled gas light was not lit and there was insufficient daylight for him to have read, even had he been able to.

Alvarez sat on the rush-seated, wooden-framed chair, the only other piece of furniture in the room. He asked how Gomez was. If God willed it, Gomez answered, he would get better, if He didn't, he would die.

'Back in the year,' said Alvarez, 'I went to the wedding of Damián and Teresa.' There was no change of expression on Gomez's leathery, lined face. 'Francisca was there. D'you know Francisca González: her husband died a long while back?'

'Died a youngster,' said Gomez, in a deep, croaky voice.

'She told us about the English señor and señorita she worked for who lived at Ca'n Ibore. Sounded a proper foreigner's mix-up – them not married, him upstairs, ill to the point of death, and her downstairs, messing around with another man.'

There was an earthenware plate on the bed and from this Gomez picked a crust of bread, spread with unrefined, greenish olive oil, from which he took a bite.

'The señor died in March. You'll remember that because you were the undertaker.'

Gomez took a second bite from the bread.

'I was surprised. I thought you'd retired a long while back.'

'Retired? Who bloody retired?'

'Isn't that what happened?'

Gomez put the bread back down on the plate. He sucked his right forefinger, carefully licking off the suspicion of olive oil which had been on it. 'I'd buried ever since my dad died and he'd buried for twenty-seven years. Clean and cheap, that's how I did it, same as my dad. Then Pablo came to the village and offered fancy coffins, fit for a king, and flowers out of season which cost a fortune. "You're nowt but a daft bugger," I told him. "People don't spend fortunes getting planted: if they've got any money they buy food for their bellies."' He coughed. 'It's me that was the daft bugger. The money was beginning and what'd been good enough for their parents wasn't good enough for them any longer. Special coffins with enough brass to build a house: flowers grown in heated greenhouses. They wanted to go out boasting.' He hawked, leaned over to spit on to the floor. 'But wait till the money stops – then see how they get buried. It'll be back to the cheapest wood and flowers what grow naturally.' He coughed again, rasping coughs which shook his body and obviously hurt. 'When they plant me I want the flowers from the mountains, like I used to see when I tended the sheep.' He closed his eyes.

'Pablo's lived in the village a long time.'

'Aye.'

'So you've not been burying regularly for years.'

'There were a few of the old ones who knew how a man should go, but when they went . . . then it was all boasting.'

'So how come you were asked to bury the English señor this spring, long after you'd given up? Why didn't they have Pablo, like everyone else?'

Without opening his eyes, Gomez picked up the bread and took a bite out of it.

'Dr Roldán came to you and asked you to do the burying, didn't he?'

'What if he did?'

'How much did he offer you to return to work for just

this once more?'

'Five thousand.'

'Come on, old man, stop lying. It was very much more than five thousand. How many hundreds of thousands was it?'

Gomez fingered the remaining piece of bread but did not eat it.

'What did you do with the money he paid you?'

'I spent it.'

Alvarez looked round the threadbare bedroom. 'On what? . . . You wouldn't put it in the bank, would you?'

'In a bank?' His voice rose. 'In the war . . .' He stopped.

'In the war,' said Alvarez quietly, 'banks were looted and the pesetas, earned by years of sweated labour, vanished. A man learned the rough way that banks aren't as safe as houses. So old an man who lived through the war would never use a bank today, even if the youngsters laugh at him and call him as daft as a March hare . . . Where have you kept that money, old man? Somewhere right close to you, where you can always feel it to make certain it hasn't vanished? Under your mattress?'

Gomez grabbed the rough blanket and the edge of the mattress underneath.

'All I want to know is, how much? Listen, would I take the money, like the bank robbers, leaving you to starve? Didn't my father know your father? Didn't you help to bury my uncle, Guillermo, who died from a broken heart after Angela was killed when she went to the Peninsula to visit her brother?'

Gomez stared wildly at Alvarez, two thin lines of spittle beginning to dribble down from the corners of his mouth.

'How much?'

'Five hundred thousand,' he whispered.

Alvarez looked round the bedroom again. Five hundred

thousand pesetas could have bought light and colour and comfort. It could have bought a new gas cooker and the food to cook on it so that Gomez's wife did not have to spend day after day bent double, tending the soil . . . But the money would stay under the mattress while the couple would continue to lead lives of poverty until perhaps it would finally be used to bury, amid the pomp and circumstance the old man so hated and despised, whomsoever of them was the last to die.

CHAPTER XXXI

Alvarez sat slumped in his office chair. He stared at the shaded light on the louvres of the closed shutters. Identity. Why had it needed the bitter hatred of a woman to show him that this case had always been about identity?

What was identity?

Individual identity arrived with birth, but what at first sight seemed automatic and unalterable was not so. A mother bore a son, but the hospital made a mistake and presented her with the wrong baby: immediately, a false identity had been established. Yet no one, if that initial mistake were not discovered and rectified, would ever suspect that the identity was false. And in time did it not really become genuine? Would the mother know her real son in twenty years' time? Would she feel the same emotional love for him as she felt for the boy she had reared, believing him to be hers? So identity was not innate, but was dependant on external events.

Identity was the past and the present, home, friends, work, habit . . . A boy went to school, got a job, started a bank account, married, bought a house, played golf on Sundays, and people knew who he was because they had seen him do some or all of these things over the years. There were papers to prove his identity. Birth and baptismal certificates, driving licence, passport, marriage certificate . . . He signed his name over and over again, continually reinforcing his claim to his identity.

But what was identity when a man left his country and arrived in a new one? Then it was not the past, but solely the present – who he claimed to be and who his papers

said he was. He could call himself Smith, Jones, or
ffoulkes-ffoulkes, provided that his papers said that was
who he was, there was money available for him in that
name, and he met no one who had known who he was
before. And thus a clever man, using the past, the present,
and the future, could have two identities, each as good as
the other, provided only that his skill at juggling did not
fail him . . .

Monica Heron had loved her husband far more deeply
than ever he, in his philandering contempt of her, had
realized. And when she had no longer been able to pretend
not to know about his infidelities she had tried to compensate for this bitter knowledge by eating. With the
bitter irony with which life has always been so generously
endowed, she had become fatter and fatter and therefore
still less desirable to him.

Eventually she had accepted the fact that she had to
bring an end to an intolerable situation. She had presented him with an ultimatum – either renounce all his
women and especially the one with whom he was now
openly having an affair, or clear out of her house, her life,
and her bank accounts.

He had no money and had been living at her expense
for far too long easily to face losing his pampered way of
life. But equally he was not prepared to lead a life in
which his only female companion was his fat, unattractive
wife . . . A classic recipe for murder.

When a mussel's thoughts turned to love, its flesh could
become poisonous, and for a reason not yet known to
science mussels which grew in some areas were potentially
more poisonous than others. In this fact Heron had seen his
chance to cut the Gordian knot. He had persuaded Betty
Stevenage to collect mussels from one of the dangerous
parts of the British coast – perhaps South Darkpoint, the

most notorious. Then he had cooked these mussels and fed them to his wife, in huge quantities because she had the appetite of a horse. Possibly Betty had had to return several times to the chosen beach and perhaps he had prepared dish after dish before he was successful in feeding her with a lethal number of mussels.

Rich wife, philandering husband, sudden death of wife ... An enquiry into the death of Monica was inevitable, but the post-mortem showed she had died from mytilo-toxin. Very regrettable, but apparently not murder.

He now had the money and everything in the garden should have been lovely, but he was not the first murderer to discover that murder didn't necessarily deliver the freedom it had seemed to promise. Betty had demanded payment for her part in the murder – faithfulness – and she had turned out to be of a very much more demand-ingly jealous nature than Monica, especially when she began to understand what should have been apparent long before, that he was constitutionally incapable of being faithful.

Murder begets murder. So Heron began to think that there would have to be a second murder, again to help him escape from a woman. But this time he would plan and execute it on his own so that he was finally free. Identity proved to be the solution to his problem of how safely to murder her.

He explained to Betty how they could never be abso-lutely certain they were safe because there was no statute of limitations for murder: a case could be re-opened after twenty years if vital evidence suddenly came to light. So they must change their identities, he first, and then even if such evidence did one day turn up, they would be beyond its consequences.

When they came to Mallorca they were Betty Stevenage

and Bill Heron – they told everyone those were their identities and they had the papers to prove it. But he had grown a very full beard, his hair was long, his movements troubled, and everyone understood that he was seriously ill. Which was why so few people ever met him and those only immediately after his arrival. No matter, Betty was there to reinforce his identity.

The money had previously taken a different route, probably ending up in Switzerland in the name of Hugh Compton. All he'd had to do to open an account was show a passport in the name of Compton (not difficult to obtain, thanks to all that money) and provide a specimen signature. From then on Hugh Compton could draw money in whatever part of the world he was in. Thanks to this arrangement, and the way in which the money Betty needed was given to her in cash, Heron when he 'died' had left nothing behind him on which the Spanish tax officials could claim their share. But he'd become a little too clever now. If he had had an account in his true name and had left in it just enough to make it seem that this was all that remained after what must have been several months of gambling, wenching and what-have-you, it would have avoided all the questions of where the inheritance had gone and where had all the sums of cash come from.

Beard shaved off, hair cut short, shoulders squared, cheek pads out, lots of health, plenty of money, a passport in the name of Hugh Compton – a new identity. He'd rented a house and set about enjoying life while his other identity, Bill Heron, lay dying upstairs in Ca'n Ibore. Not for the first time, he'd unwisely enjoyed life too much: identity might change but character didn't. Inevitably Betty had become more and more jealous and time after time she must have taxed him with being unfaithful while she stayed in Ca'n Ibore to lend verisimilitude to the deception, time after time he must have tried to reassure her that all he was doing was creating a character totally removed from the stricken Bill Heron, not actually living it.

Alvarez bent down and opened the bottom right-hand drawer of the desk. He brought out a bottle of brandy and a glass, filled the glass, and drank.

Betty, a woman of not very keen intelligence, had from the beginning fallen into the trap of believing that she could keep Compton's love with her body, little realizing that he was a man who sharply differentiated between lust and love and that his lust could only be satiated by novelty. She had demanded that he frequently return to Ca'n Ibore so they could make physical love. He must have tried to refuse, realizing the dangers of such visits, but she had been able to blackmail him into going. He would have gone at night and sometimes stayed until the next night, taking the chance during the day to become Bill Heron so that Francisca could see or hear him and later be a witness as to his declining state of health. (The shutters in the bedroom had been drawn, the bedclothes up about him, so all she had really seen had been a false beard and a mop of hair.) The day she had turned up unexpectedly in the evening and had heard Betty speaking words of passion and love must have made him frightened and furious and determined to kill her as soon as possible.

The aconite had been at least sixteen months old and he had needed to make certain it was still effective, not having the specialized knowledge to know whether or not its potency deteriorated with time. So, with the same degree of callousness as he had shown previously, he had poisoned the dog. Francisca had been horrified that Betty could weep frantic tears for the dog and not for the dying

Heron. A clever man would have understood the real significance of the facts.

Obviously, the major problem to be solved before Heron could carry out all his plans had been that when he 'died' a doctor would have to certify his death and the 'body' would have to be buried. Where to find a doctor who would agree to fake the death? Heron could clearly judge his fellows in the broadest sense, yet equally clearly would usually miss any finer shades of character. Dr Roldán loved money, to the extent that a career which had started as a mission soon became solely a means of personal gain, and therefore the offer of a million pesetas for issuing a false death certificate was bound to attract him. But beyond that point Heron had made a very serious mistake in not realizing that Roldán would lie in the course of his work, if paid enough, but he would never betray that work.

Gomez, the undertaker, was a far simpler man who for years had been suffering under a personal grievance. Thus when he was offered half a million pesetas to carry out a faked burial, he saw his proposed reward as two-fold – the money and the secret satisfaction of knowing that the new undertaker who had usurped his job would never earn nearly so much for just one burial.

Heron had 'died'. Now each of them became deeply concerned with his or her own problem.

His problem. How to cover up the coming murder of Betty? When a body suffered serious decomposition, the poison aconite could not be isolated and identified: so her body needed to be hidden for as long as possible. The landlord of Ca'n Ibore was a man who pursued every last peseta with fanatical perseverance and because of this had refused to carry out even the most essential repairs to the house. Thus what could appear more natural by way of retaliation than to leave the house locked up and denied to him until the last day of the lease? In the heat, decomposition would be very quick. What's more, the mechanics of the plan would be carried out by Betty herself, further allaying suspicion.

Her problem. To identify the woman he was currently chasing and to force him to leave her. Betty knew he was seeing Diana quite often and that there was another man in Diana's life, Harry Waynton, but she couldn't be certain of the degrees of relationship. So she went out of her way to become friendly with Waynton in the hope that she would learn the facts and also through him be able to keep some sort of tab on what Hugh Compton was doing. But because she dared not ask any questions directly, she had always had to put them in a very roundabout way. That was why, in the square, she had asked Waynton whether Diana were seeing Alex Dunton or Gordon Elliott. When one learned that Betty had had a lover, it had been natural to suppose that she had been jealously interested in who those two men were seeing, but in fact her interest had been in who Diana was seeing and she had only introduced their names because she knew Diana would not have been seeing them and had hoped that because of this Waynton would have told her whom Diana *was* seeing. A clever man must surely have realized this, once he became satisfied that the two men never had been friends of Diana?

Accidental death gradually assumed the sinister mantle of murder and when it did so Compton's one really serious mistake came home to roost. Roldán, who had connived in falsifying a death because this harmed no one, discovered to his horror that he had been an accessory, no matter if unknowingly and indirectly, in what now appeared to have been a murder. He was a doctor, not a murderer. He had threatened Compton with exposure and because of that had had to be killed. Gomez knew only that Roldán had given him half a million pesetas to perform a false burial and so he had been allowed to go on living.

Denise Roldán had known that her husband had had contact with a rich Englishman called Compton and that something about this relationship had suddenly worried her husband most terribly. So when she learned that her dead husband had had in his possession about a million pesetas which couldn't be accounted for, that he had probably been murdered, that his murder was directly connected with the money . . .

Her emotions had always been intense and she had loved Rodriguez Roldán to a degree not known, perhaps fortunately, to many. And so, because hate was the opposite face to love, she had hated his murderer with savage intensity. She could have denounced Compton, but then punishment would have been in the hands of the law and the law didn't always extract the last ounce of retribution. She wanted revenge to be complete. So she hid her desperate sorrow and returned to the world, like any other widow who wasn't really very sorry that her husband had died, and she had made certain that she met Compton. She was uniquely beautiful, he had never been able to resist a beautiful woman. So when she suggested they leave the island together . . .

Somewhere, Denise was fooling Compton into believing she loved him passionately as she bided her time before she extracted her revenge for the murder of her husband . . . Alvarez shivered. Such a woman would recognize no limits.

After a while, he reached over for the telephone directory and searched through it to find out how to make an international call. Then, making certain he had ready the telephone number of the Bearstone County Constabulary HQ, he dialled the international exchange, got the carry-on tone, and dialled the English number.

A woman answered and he asked for Detective-Inspector Fletcher, adding that this was an international call so could she be as quick as possible.

As he waited, he pictured the detective-inspector, immaculately presented, the embodiment of smart efficiency. On his face would be the self-confident, vaguely patronizing and superior expression which could so annoy an ignorant foreigner who hadn't had the advantage of having been born an Englishman . . .

'Fletcher speaking.'

'Good morning, señor. This is Enrique Alvarez.'

'Hullo, there. How are you? And how's the weather with you?'

'Very hot and sunny for the time of year.'

'Really? It's raining here.' Somehow he managed to suggest that rain was to be preferred, if it fell in England.

'Señor, do you remember that when I was in England we discussed the case of Señora Heron? She was the wife of . . .'

'Died from mytilotoxin poisoning after eating a large quantity of mussels. Spanish mussels.'

How in the name of hell did the man remember everything? 'Señor, I have to tell you now that I think perhaps her death was not accidental. The poison aconite . . .'

There was a short, sarcastic laugh. 'I'll give you full marks for perseverance, old man, but I really do think you'll have to return to the facts. You seem to be forgetting that there was a post-mortem, conducted by Professor Keen. Naturally, I can't say what goes on in other countries although one gains a rough idea at times, but here we can place complete reliance on the findings of a pathologist. There's no question but that Mrs Heron died from mytilotoxin poisoning.'

'Indeed, and it was never my intention to question the findings of one of your eminent pathologists. It was of Señor Heron's illness I was going to speak. You will understand that it is only with diffidence I ask this, but did you ever request that tests be made to discover exactly from what form of poisoning the señor had suffered?'

'Why?'

'It occurred to me that perhaps if he had deliberately secured a supply of mussels from a place such as South Darkpoint, where they are known to become poisonous during the breeding season, and had he fed these to his wife in order to kill her, he would have been reluctant to eat the mussels himself as he would not have known how many might prove fatal to him. So might he not have made certain what was a non-fatal dose of aconite and taken that, since the symptoms of the two illnesses are so similar? . . . But knowing how superbly you managed the case, I thought that almost certainly you could assure me the test had been made so that this possibility should be immediately forgotten.'

There was a long silence. Alvarez leaned forward to refill his glass. The gecko suddenly scampered into sight round the corner of the window and he winked at it.